EASIER DEAD THAN ALIVE

Lt. Stowe watched the men, stripped naked, being lashed to poles so that their feet hung aimlessly above the ground. He watched the warriors, each with a sharp piece of flint in hand, form a single file and slowly circle around the dangling men.

He saw the circling figures suddenly dart out of line, saw them rake their flint down the bodies of the bound men, over and over again until it was better to shut his eyes and see nothing more.

When he could finally look again, he was being led away by two smiling warriors. He knew they were saving him for something special, and that he would soon understand that there are some things worse than death.

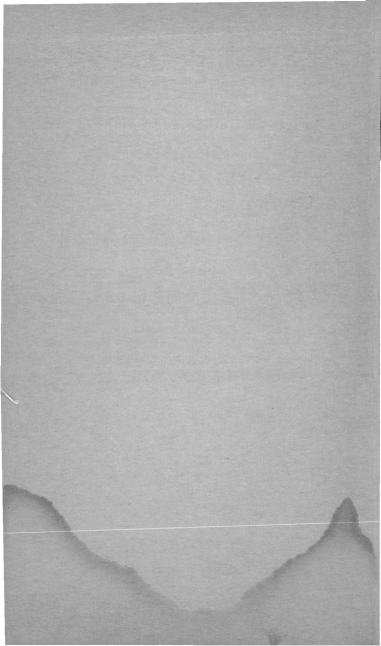

TEXAS,
BLOOD RED

Shepard Rifkin

PaperJacks LTD.

TORONTO   NEW YORK

PaperJacks

TEXAS, BLOOD RED

PaperJacks LTD

330 STEELCASE RD. E., MARKHAM, ONT. L3R 2M1
210 FIFTH AVE., NEW YORK, N.Y. 10010

PaperJacks edition published September 1987

ISBN 0-7701-0686-2

TEXAS,
BLOOD RED

ONE

In the early seventies military buckboards had few springs, and Lt. Samuel Stowe had come ninety miles from railhead in one. He had been quiet, but Mr. Albert Cross, the new Indian Agent going out to replace John Pease, had been making speeches against Texas. The sergeant assigned to bring them to the Fort was listening with pleasure. Sgt. Christie could hardly wait to get to work on Mr. Cross.

"This country," said Cross, "looks like the skin of a diseased dog; and last night I bought an apple and they charged me a quarter for it. A quarter!" He was furious. He took off his hat and ran a handkerchief over his bald head.

"Mr. Cross," said the sergeant, in the interests of truth, "they come all the way from Arkansas."

"Well, why don't some people plant a few trees? That's easy."

"Mr. Cross," said the sergeant, "to tell you the truth, I been in Texas ten years, and I ain't seen a single apple tree nowheres in Texas."

"And the heat!" Cross said. It was August. The lieutenant stirred restlessly. The sergeant could see Lt. Stowe was bored with Mr. Cross.

The sergeant was big, a little fat, and strong. He looked perpetually mournful, as if he were on the edge of tears, and he had been nicknamed "Boo-Hoo" Christie, shortened to "Boo." He was sweating, and from time to time he looked mournfully at the ridges that overlooked the road. Lt. Stowe noticed the glances. Finally he asked, "What're you looking for, Sergeant?"

Sgt. Christie debated the wisdom of telling a horrible lie, but decided to tell the truth. He had seen the lieutenant's transfer papers. This lieutenant was no kid from the Point, but had been through the war and had been promoted on the field.

"There's a couple Comanche bands heard of the reservation and the treaty but they don't like the idea," said the sergeant. "They like horses and they like scalps."

"And we got both?" asked the lieutenant, seriously, but the sergeant caught the slight smile. Christie decided he liked the lieutenant.

"Yes, sir," said the sergeant. "The horses ain't so good, and you and I got regulation short haircuts so we won't hang in no lodges, but sometimes these Comanches ain't particular." He stared at Mr. Cross's bald head, which was shiny as a brass door-knob. Cross reddened.

They were all silent. The buckboard rattled across a shallow broad creek, swung up between two cliffs that hugged the road, and turned to the left. Twelve mounted Indians were waiting there. Eight of them had their rifles pointing at the buckboard. The lieutenant took a deep breath and the sergeant said softly, "Better not move, Lieutenant. How do you know they ain't Osage?"

The lieutenant relaxed. "They ain't, though," added the sergeant. "They're Comanches."

"Run for it!" said Cross.

"Take a look backwards," said the sergeant. There were ten warriors walking their horses two hundred feet in the rear. "We're boxed in," said the sergeant, almost cheerfully.

"Sergeant," asked the lieutenant, "What do you say? Shall we make a run for it?"

"Lieutenant, there're eighteen of 'em. I move we listen." He pulled the buckboard to a halt.

The leader rode out. His war bonnet fell down to his hips in a gorgeous blaze of red and white. He wore nothing but a breechclout and moccasins with leggings that came to his knees. His empty right hand was held high, palm forward.

"Better keep your hands in your lap, Lieutenant, and show they're empty," said the sergeant. "You too, Mr. Cross. I don't wanna die on a hot day in Texas because of a misunderstanding." They put their hands in their laps.

The chief began talking sign. His face was flat as a dish, and a big curved nose jutted out. His lips were thin and tight. He wore silver buttons sewed on to his leggings in a vertical row, and Lt. Stowe saw they were Mexican coins that had been pounded flat and then bent into a slight curve. On the flanks of several of the horses he saw the brand, "3rd US."

"Yeah, Lieutenant, I see that too," said the sergeant. "What do you want me to do, sue 'em? They was stolen a couple weeks ago, right from the meadows by the Fort."

The Indian finished making sign. Christie nodded. The Indians grinned, wheeled their horses, and began to walk them across the prairie to the north. The band in back of the buckboard joined them. None of them looked back.

"That was Yellow Bird, with the bonnet," said Christie. "He's a war chief. He said he led the band that stole the horses. All he wanted this powwow for was to tell me that he hoped the next lot would be better."

"I'll tell you the way to handle Indians like that," said Cross. "You shoot 'em first, and powwow later."

"Sure," said the sergeant soothingly. "I told him he

was always welcome to shop around the corral, though."
He looked after the Comanches. "That's the first time
I've seen Yellow Bird lookin' like he did. Sour and sort
of burnin' underneath. But it's been buildin' up for a couple of years. Pease was able to keep it under control, but
now—I dunno," and he looked directly at Cross.

"Up in Wisconsin we handle 'em differently," said
Cross. "They come into the Agency and we make 'em
be respectful and respect Government property. I don't
know too much about how you people are running things
down here, but these Indians are just bluffing you. That's
obvious."

"Well, Mr. Cross," said the sergeant, "you only just
seen your first Comanche and you already know how to
handle them. I been fightin' 'em and watchin' 'em for
ten years and I still don't know which way they'll jump."

Cross looked at him narrowly. "Let me tell the
experience I've had," he said. "A friend of mine was the
agent with the Ogallala Sioux and he was talking one
night with Spotted Tail, an Ogallala chief. He told my
friend he had been asked by the Missouri River Sioux how
it was that the Ogallalas, who had been opposin' the
government for years, always got more rations than
themselves, who had been at peace for years. He said,
he told me, 'You Indians on the Missouri are too good.
Why don't you take off the white men's breeches you
are wearing, put on a breechclout, a little paint, howl a
little, get brave, and the white man will give you plenty
to eat?' I tell you, they're bluffin'."

"Sure, Mr. Cross," said the sergeant. "Now you just
calm down and we'll be in the Fort soon and you can
make your speech all over again to the major. He's pretty
new around here. He's only been here four years and he'd
appreciate your advice. The lieutenant here is new to
Texas and it ain't no use talkin' to him because he's so
confused he'd forget. And it's no use talkin' to me
because I'm old and stubborn, and set in my ways, like.
So enjoy the scenery, which, like you say, looks like a
dog with the mange, while I figure out where'll we plant

all the apple trees you want to see planted out here along the trail to save haulin' from Arkansas.''

Cross got the point. He set his jaw and looked with disgust at the tumbleweeds a sudden hot wind sent bouncing and skipping across the road. The sergeant looked at the lieutenant. He liked the way the lieutenant had behaved. He had been all ready to go for his gun, the sergeant noticed, and by the way he had placed his feet on the footrest the sergeant knew he was prepared to tumble flat into the wagon after his first shot and fight from behind his trunk. And now that danger was over the lieutenant did not, like most men, talk and laugh too much.

''I tell you one thing, Lieutenant,'' said the sergeant. ''Lucky for us they were in a good mood. They probably just counted coup somewheres and every one got his share, so none of 'em was feelin' bad. If they hadn't gotten away with our ponies I bet they would've jumped us, even though they weren't wearing war paint.''

''I thought they always put on war paint when they meant business.''

''There's no law says they gotta, Lieutenant. And especially now, when the chiefs are comin' together from far north as the Platte, and it's been pretty hot and the hunting's been bad—they're touchy. They ain't gonna like the new treaty and they know it and we know it. And it's awful easy to pull a trigger when you're hot and touchy and ridin' a fast pony. Their rifles are sort of old and they can't get ammunition easy and when they do get it they don't often waste it practicing, but if they get worked up enough . . .''

The sergeant watched the lieutenant rub his chin, feeling the red stubble.

''If you want to freshen up and shave, Lieutenant, there's a ranch a couple miles before the fort.'' The lieutenant smiled and nodded.

Cross said, ''There'll be plenty of time for that when we get to the Fort.''

''You're right,'' the sergeant agreed, pleasantly, ''but

this is a military vehicle with two military fellers aboard. And the lieutenant commands in military territory. And where does the lieutenant want to go?"

"The ranch," said Lt. Stowe.

"So we gotta go to the ranch," Sgt. Christie said. Cross looked at him. The sergeant stared calmly back. The sergeant weighed almost two hundred pounds, Cross about the same, and both were in their late thirties. Both were still powerful men. Cross's big right hand came up and he gently felt his black mustache. He was thinking.

In a few minutes they reached the ranch and swung in. They stopped in front of a low adobe building with six-inch square windows. In those days ranch houses were a combination of home and a fort. A woman came out of the door and shaded her eyes.

"Hello, Mrs. Anson," said the sergeant. He climbed down, and when he was near her he said, "Can this young 'un wash up so's he can make a good impression on Major Welles?"

"He sure can," said Mrs. Anson. The lieutenant climbed down and the three walked into the house. Cross remained on the buckboard, stroking his mustache and wiping his face. "Don't the other gentleman want to set a while where it's cool?" she asked.

"He don't want to do nothin' except the opposite of what we wanna do," said the sergeant, "so I guess he's happy out there."

Mrs. Anson began to heat some water. "Where's Mr. Anson and the boys?" asked the sergeant.

"Oh," she said placidly, "over to San Anselmo." She fetched two towels. "I'm all right here," she said. She pointed behind the door. Three carbines lay against the wall.

The two men drank thirstily from a clay jug that hung from the porch roof. Mrs. Anson took the hot water off the fire and poured it into a basin. Then she went out and sat on the porch.

"I don't think he's gonna be happy here," said the sergeant, watching the lieutenant lather his face.

"What's wrong with the other agent?"

"Now that's sad," said the sergeant. "Pease is—well, he's fine. Only he's being transferred. Department politics, I bet. Maybe Cross got bigger friends in Washington. The Comanches don't like the idea because they get along fine with him. It's a hard thing, dealing with Indians, and especially Comanches, and I don't think this Cross-Cut Saw here has the right touch, somehow. Particularly since he knows all about Comanches, he says.

"They like Pease a lot. They been coming in for the last three weeks to make a big talk against the transfer. Mr. Cross ain't gonna be happy here at all. He might get so unhappy he could ask his big friends to be transferred again, or the Comanches could make some excitement down in the Panhandle and ask again for Pease, and maybe the Department might go insane and ship Pease back again. Maybe. Where'd you get that scar, Lieutenant?"

"Which one?" The lieutenant was bare to the waist, and he twisted his tall thin brown torso to see where the sergeant was pointing.

"That one way down on your back." A long white scar ran straight across his back, just missing the spine.

"Oh," he said, turning back again to shave, "Chickamauga."

"Looks like a saber cut."

"It is," said the lieutenant, concentrating on shaving his upper lip. "My horse broke his leg and I was getting out from under and the next thing I knew a southern gentleman gave me a scar for my grandchildren to look at someday."

The sergeant sat astride an old chair and leaned his jaw on his clasped hands. "Where you from, Lieutenant?"

"Cherry Valley. New York State."

"Pretty country? Green and plenty of water?"

The lieutenant stopped shaving and looked at the sergeant in the mirror. The sergeant's jaw was big as half a brick. "Yes. And plenty of apples."

"Tell me about your apples. I love to hear about apples, now that Johnny Apples out there can't hear you, Lieutenant."

"Well," said the lieutenant, looking up dreamily at the ceiling, where rows of onions hung Mexican style, "we have great big apples, big as your two fists. And we have apples with white flecks on them, like on a deer. Pretty as a little deer—you'd hate to eat them. And apples as red as your best girl's cheek when you'd rub it with snow."

"Man," said the sergeant, "I really do miss apples." He stood up. "You look fine, Lieutenant. Major Welles is rough on brand-new lieutenants." They walked outside.

"What do we owe you, Mrs. Anson?" asked Lieutenant Stowe.

"Some apples, some day," she said, smiling, "when they grow in Texas."

The two men thanked her and walked out. "I'm rough on brand-new lieutenants, too," said Sergeant Christie, "but that could have been my brother that whacked you at Chickamauga."

"Oh."

"Yep," added the sergeant, "or my uncle. We're from 'sippi." He swung up into the buckboard, lightly.

The lieutenant climbed up and looked at him. "Whoever did it had a heavy hand," he said.

"We all weigh over two hundred," said the sergeant, clicking his tongue at the horses.

"He should have come at me with the point," said the lieutenant.

"You still talking about the Civil War?" asked Cross.

"Please," said the sergeant, "the War for the Southern Confederacy."

"I don't go along with that nonsense," said Cross,

thirsty and angry. "We say 'Civil War' and we'll always say it."

"Where'd you spend the war, Mr. Cross?" asked the lieutenant.

"I had a very responsible position in Minneapolis buying grain for the Union Armies."

"How far is that from Chickamauga?" asked the sergeant.

"Where's Chickamauga?"

"Here's one that won't forget," said the lieutenant, "and if the sergeant wants it to be the 'War for the Southern Confederacy', why, that's what it was, come to think of it."

"It's been a nice ride, Lieutenant Stowe and Mr. Cross," said the sergeant, "and if you look ahead, down at the foot of the bluffs . . ."

From the edge of the red bluffs that looked down on the Fort they could see everything at once. There was the Fort with the stockade around it, the stables, the corrals, the rows of houses where the NCO's lived. Because there was always washing being dried on the lines by the NCO's wives, it was called Suds Row.

Most of the Comanches were on the reservation and they came in in the spring for their clothes and their tobacco. There the Red River flowed slow and easy along a sandy bottom; in the rich sandy loam of the river banks sunflowers grew fifteen feet tall in the shade of the cottonwoods. The Comanche girls were swimming in the river after their work for the day. From far up the bluffs they could hear them laughing and see them splash water at one another. Along the river were the flats, and there the young men were racing their horses. They practiced riding in pairs, reaching down to rescue a wounded or dismounted warrior. The women had pegged down fresh buffalo hides and they were scraping, getting them ready for the traders; little girls were playing with tiny buckskin tents, putting little buckskin dolls into them, and the older children were hitching a toy travois to a patient dog. Then they looked farther, and saw the meadows ablaze with big yellow bees, and on the mountains there were plenty of elk and blacktail deer, and at the foot of the mountains there were whitetail deer.

There were still buffalo then, and in the fall the traders would come for their robes. But the ranches were pushing up from the south, and what with the buffalo going, every once in a while a Comanche would kill a steer because he was hungry. Then the owners of the steer would get mad and come to the Agency and complain. There were troubles. It was not as good as it was before the whites came into Texas but there was still hope among the older Indians that somehow the buffalo would be there forever, and that the railroad would not come, and that the ranches would stop moving up into Comanche country and that treaties would be kept. The younger warriors, though, were talking and acting like war.

They watched the young Comanches sit their fast ponies atop the bluff, smelling the sage grass. And Sgt. Christie knew that the young men were probably dreaming of stealing horses from the Osage, or from the ranchers, or, even better, if they were lucky and brave and good medicine was with them, from the Third Cavalry.

As the wagon eased down the slope some of the braves raced by, calling to one another.

The sergeant looked after them, angry, and then shrugged.

Lt. Stowe asked what they had said.

"They cussed us some," said the sergeant, "but that don't bother me so much. What bothers me is that they're takin' to talkin' like that all of a sudden. And Comanches don't just fight with their mouths. They back it up with rifles. I don't like it too much."

They rode the rest of the way in silence. Some of the braves smelled the roasting meat, and they wheeled their ponies and cantered down through the meadows and splashed through the shallows where some of the younger squaws were still swimming.

TWO

The Administrative Building of Fort Brill was a small affair, built of adobe, fronting the river so as to catch any breeze that might blow northward up the slope. It had a porch that ran along its entire front, and on it were two rocking chairs where the major and his daughter sat on cool evenings. From the west side a gentle slope led down to a large field; its absolutely bare surface pitted with hoofmarks showed that was where cavalry maneuvers were held.

Lt. Stowe walked up the slope from the corral, Sgt. Christie alongside. "Maybe I better give you a little hint," said the sergeant, "Major Welles—he's like Grant was."

The delicacy of the statement amused the lieutenant. "You mean he drinks?"

"Yep," said the sergeant, relieved that he didn't have to put it into words. "He's been off on a high lonesome for three days now, they tell me, and he'll jump you for a nothing."

"I'll watch my step," said Lt. Stowe. He had the warm, comfortable feeling that he had been adopted by his sergeant. They walked across the porch and opened a door marked, *"Commanding Officer Third Cavalry."*

The blinds had been drawn against the sun, and in the dimness it took a few seconds before the lieutenant could make out the interior. There was a small desk against the wall. Next to it, under the windows, were two long wooden benches where two bored troopers were sitting. Next to them sat a short fat civilian. At the desk sat a young, short lieutenant with blonde hair. A small sign on his desk said, *"Lt. Wynn Adjutant."* He rose when he saw Lt. Stowe. The sergeant looked sternly at the men on the bench. They rose wearily and stood at a bored attention. "Lieutenant Wynn," said Sgt. Christie, "This here is Lieutenant Stowe. Salute and sit down," he said, glowering at the troopers.

They saluted and sat down. The lieutenants shook hands. "Glad you're here," said Lt. Wynn. "The major'll be out in a second."

"How's he feeling?" asked Sgt. Christie.

Lt. Wynn raised his eyes to the ceiling and murmured, "He just came back from three days at San Anselmo." One of the troopers grinned.

"What happened?" asked the sergeant, walking over to the troopers. They spoke quietly, but Lt. Stowe could hear them.

"Pulling the town up by its roots don't help the town none," said one of the troopers. "The sheriff said he was going to write to Washington about the way the major behaved." The trooper looked proud.

The door to the major's office burst open. The troopers jumped to their feet and stood at rigid attention. The major came in. He was a tall man of fifty; his black hair was close-cropped and beginning to grey. He had a hangover. "You the new lieutenant?" he asked. The lieutenant saluted and held out his travel orders. "Yes, sir," he began, "Lieutenant Stowe reporting . . ."

"One minute, Lieutenant," said the major, politely enough. He said, "Lieutenant Wynn, come in."

Lt. Wynn followed. Through the half-opened door

those in the office outside heard him say, "You got some liniment for my throat? Some son of a bitch kicked me there last time I was in San Anselmo, and it's acting up."

"I think there's some in your drawer, sir," said Lt. Wynn. The troopers grinned, listening. There was the rattle and squeak of a drawer opening and closing. "Here are Lt. Stowe's travel papers," Lt. Wynn said. "He . . ."

"Nemmind that nonsense," said the major. "I can read." There was a brief rustle of papers. Then he came out.

"If you'll wait a moment, Lieutenant Stowe," he said, "till I get rid of this daily nonsense. All right, Wheaton," he began, "what stupid thing did you do now?"

The adjutant stood up and pulled out a sheet from the pile of dispatches, orders of the day, requisitions, and notices piled on his desk. He began reading. "Private Wheaton, on KP duty, purposely broke a china plate, saying quote he would break many more to get relieved from this damn place unquote."

"That true, Wheaton?" asked the major.

"Yessir!" said Wheaton.

"I feel the same way," said the major. "Five dollars fine, carry a thirty pound log six hours a day for fifteen days, and don't break any more Government china. Next?"

"Private Kelly, sir, ordered to get salt for the mules, said quote to hell with the mules unquote."

"That true, Kelly?"

Pvt. Kelly turned red and said, "Yessir."

"Ten dollars fine. Dismiss and report to your corporal. Next."

"Mr. Albertson, Fort dairyman, sir. On Thursday last, when the twenty-four pound field gun was fired . . ."

"Oh, God, my head," said the major. He sat down on the bench and rubbed his forehead.

The door opened and a girl walked in. "Hi, Dad," she said. "I hear you've been bad."

"I've been terrible, Beth."

She said, "Come into your office a minute." He got up and they went into the office.

Lt. Stowe stared after her. She was almost as tall as he was, and she had black hair that came 'way down past her shoulders. He had seen a field of wheat get going in a soft spring wind, that slow wave that wheat has, and that was how her hair came down, he thought. She was all tanned, like an Indian girl. Her hair had the blue-black look of thunderclouds in a spring lightning storm: blue-black and shining, as if there were a light shining from 'way inside. But her eyes were blue. Not the blue of a robin's egg, thought the Lieutenant—that would be too pale. And not as blue as plums—that would be too blue. They were the kind of blue, he decided, that he used to see on the first really beautiful day of the year—the kind of day that comes in late April in Cherry Valley when all of a sudden he knew that the last snow had come, that the last cold rain had gone, that from then on the cherry trees would bloom up and down the valley. There was a small flush under her brown cheeks, like the cheeks of Mexican girls.

He had no idea what his face was showing until the sergeant said, "We think so too, Lieutenant."

"Ummm," said the lieutenant, reddening.

The door opened again and the major came out, making a face. He was working his mouth, as if he had just swallowed something nasty. She was patting him on the back. She wore a short skirt, and Lt. Stowe noticed that she wore leggings that came to her knees, like the Indian girls. "Lieutenant Stowe," said Lt. Wynn, "Miss Welles." The lieutenant's blush deepened. "How do you do, Ma'am," he said.

"Didn't you ever see leggings before?" she asked sharply.

"Didn't mean to stare, Ma'am," he said.

"The lieutenant's new to Indian country, Miss Welles," said the sergeant. She sat down on the bench while the major wrote a few lines on a report. She stretched out her long legs, crossed her tanned arms and stared coolly at Lt. Stowe.

She thought he was like the other lieutenants that came out to the Fort. He looked at her, she thought, like they all did, with big eyes that said, "I wish you would go to bed with me and maybe, if I'm lucky, maybe you will." But he wasn't a pretty boy, she thought, and that was a point in his favor. And she could see that Boo liked him. That was something else in his favor. Boo didn't like any of the lieutenants on the post and never had. The lieutenant was a year or so older than she was, and she liked that. She was older than the other lieutenants, and it was nice, she thought, to feel younger for a change. She liked the way he blushed when she snapped at him for looking at her leggings. She figured out that if he had been in the Army for four years he must have gone in when he was sixteen. That meant he had volunteered. She liked that. And four more years at the Point gave him eight in the Army. That meant all he had ever known was Army, and she smiled, because that meant he was almost an Army brat, like she was.

His face was too long, she thought, and so was his nose, and so was his upper lip, but his greenish eyes went well with his red hair. His ears were really too big. But he stood well, she thought. Straight, almost like a Comanche brave, but not stiff, the silly way they teach them at the Point.

His hands were big, and a white scar ran across the knuckles of his right hand. There was a sort of red fuzz on the backs of his hands, but his fingernails were clean, and he smelled of soap.

She watched him looking at her father. She watched him to see if he was laughing at Major Welles for being drunk last night. But he was polite and attentive. There was a tiny smile at the corners of his lips, but she was sure it had nothing to do with her father. She thought it was there because he liked her and the Fort and Texas.

It would be nice, she thought, showing him the tepees

and teaching him sign talk and the valleys where they hunted antelope on Sundays. Her thoughts were interrupted by her father.

The major looked up from his finished report. "All right, dairyman," he said. "What's the story?"

"Three days ago," began the adjutant, "the major ordered the new field artillery piece fired to impress the chiefs. The shell landed in a meadow a mile away and killed a cow, by accident."

"Were the chiefs impressed?"

"Very, sir."

"Who aimed the gun?"

After a long pause the adjutant spoke. "I did, sir."

"Thirty dollars fine for being stupid, reduced to fifteen because of the good impression on the chiefs. How much your cow worth, dairyman?"

"Sixty-five dollars."

"Put in a claim for forty and I'll pass it. Otherwise, I'll keep writing across your claim the word 'excessive'."

The dairyman sighed. "All right, Major." He went out sadly.

"What did I tell you, Lieutenant?" whispered the sergeant. "Business gets done fast around here."

"Sergeant!"

"Sir!"

"See that Wheaton walks his six hours between ten and four. And don't give him any water during his little excursion."

"Yes, sir."

"All right, dismiss." The sergeant saluted, spun around, winked at the lieutenant and left. The major still held Lt. Stowe's orders in his hand. He read them again, while Beth looked him over coolly. "Fresh out of the Point?"

"Yes, sir."

"Rather old for that, aren't you?"

"Yes, sir. I went in after four years in the Army."

"Oh yes, I see it now. Commissioned on the field, at Seven Pines. All right, then. I figured you were wet behind the ears and I was going to give you a little speech we give our lieutenants but you've seen active service. Just get along well with your sergeant, which you know already. Forget most of what you learned at the Point, but I suppose you know that too."

The door opened and Cross walked in with a stocky, ugly little man who needed a shave.

"Mr. Pease," said Beth, her voice warm with pleasure. The lieutenant wondered if she would ever talk to him like that.

"Major, Beth," said the little man, "I want to introduce Mr. Cross, the new agent." Cross nodded, then he wrinkled his nose as he caught the smell of alcohol on the major's breath.

"Mr. Cross, sir," said the major. "It's a shame you're coming in at a time like this, when the Comanches are bitter about Mr. Pease's transfer. But we'll try and make it as easy for you as we can. Most of the chiefs are reasonable, and I'm pretty sure we can smooth the situation over. The big trouble is," said the major, sitting down beside Beth and stretching out his long legs, "they don't understand that people can be transferred. They just don't want him transferred, and they're sending their best talkers."

"There's no reason you have to give them any explanation at all," said Cross. "This constant babying of the Indians is ridiculous. I never tolerated it at my Agency."

Where was that, sir?" asked Pease, mildly.

"Deer Lake."

"Isn't that the Northern Chippewa Agency?"

Cross nodded. Pease went on. "Wisconsin?" Cross nodded again, "Yes," he said, "and we laid down the rules, and that was that."

"Comanches are different from Chippewas," said Pease, quietly.

"Nonsense! They're all dirty, and they all get drunk, and their women are diseased."

"Chippewas are forest Indians," said Pease, softly. "Their reservation is completely surrounded by white settlements. Railroads go clear through their territory. If they went on the warpath, how would they eat? Get ammunition? Find room to maneuver? Soldiers could be there in one day. They know it and they're resigned.

"But as for the Comanches: no railroads. Only one regiment at the Fort. Their country stretches for hundreds of miles north and west—no soldiers, no settlements. They live off the country as they travel. There's buffalo and water. They have horses.

"The young braves are coming up now, the ones who were too young to have a voice in council the day the older chiefs voted to surrender and come onto the reservation. When they speak we listen. They know their power. And some of the young chiefs may go on the warpath if you just look at them the wrong way. That is why the major and I feel that the transfer has come at the wrong time.

"I am due to leave in a week, Mr. Cross, and I should like to show you around and tell you as much as I can so that you will make a good impression at the talks on Sunday."

Cross looked bored, then irritated, as Pease was speaking. "I don't like being spoken to as if I was an idiot child," he said angrily. "I got common sense and that's all I need in any situation. I don't want to go to school again just so's you can feel important. Now, will you give me the keys to your office so I can clean out your stuff and get goin'?" He held out his hand.

"Mr. Cross," said Pease, flushing, "I am not due to be relieved till Monday morning at eight o'clock. That is when you will get your keys."

The major spoke. "Mr. Cross, perhaps Mr. Pease did give you the impression that he was a schoolteacher. I am sure he did not intend to. Did you, Mr. Pease?"

"No, Major," said Pease. He set his teeth.

"Well," said the major, "Mr. Pease has said he's sorry, haven't you, Mr. Pease?"

"Yes, sir," said Pease quietly.

"So, now, Mr. Cross," the major went on, "let me urge you to listen to Mr. Pease, as he suggested. He did not say so, but he knows the Comanches as well as any one in Texas. He even married one of their women and he is completely trusted by the tribe. A good word from him before you take office will be just about the best thing you could start with, Mr. Cross."

Cross stared at him. "First, Major, I resent being treated like an idiot. Pease didn't apologize to me. Second, any agent who goes around marryin' squaws— Washington oughta know about that. Third . . . ," he wrinkled his nose, "I'll be over on Monday at eight o'clock." He turned and walked out.

"Want me to get 'im?" asked Sgt. Christie. Major Welles shook his head. The sergeant turned to Pease. "How about you, Joe? Say so . . ."

"No," said Pease. "I've got a feeling he's going to get plenty before he's finished here."

He sat down beside the major and Beth. The major looked up. "Sergeant," he said, "show the lieutenant his quarters."

"I already showed them to him, sir. Listen, Major, I can catch him behind the stables . . ."

"That's enough. Show the lieutenant the corral and the barracks."

The sergeant and the lieutenant saluted and walked out. Across the field they could see the figure of Cross sauntering toward the river. A small cloud of cigar smoke hung above him.

"I know just what that son of a bitch of a Johnny Apples is gonna do," said the sergeant.

"What, Sergeant?"

"He's gonna try and get a peep at the naked squaws

swimmin', and I hope to God a brave knifes him."

"No such luck," said the lieutenant. "That kind lives forever."

"In Texas," said the sergeant, happily, "things are arranged different."

THREE

All that afternoon and all the next day the dirty white cones of the tepees rose around Fort Brill. The Comanches were coming in from as far west as Concho, as far north as the Cimarron, as far south as the big ranches had pushed up (Big Springs), and as far east as the Washita.

The heat got worse. On the field Lt. Stowe and his troop practiced maneuvers: trot, gallop, and charge! The horses sweated and gasped in the heat; when they began to shudder and tremble Sgt. Christie said, "Lieutenant, I guess we better slow up here, and wait till the sun goes down."

The lieutenant nodded. He, too, was panting. "Troop, dismount!" he ordered. "Walk your horses and then water them."

They sat down in the shade of the stables. In front of them Pvt. Wheaton was walking his punishment tour. Each time he had paced his fifty steps, he would shift the thirty pound log to his other shoulder, spit angrily, and start to walk back again.

The lieutenant got up and walked to the corner of the stable, where a clay jug hung from the overhang of the sloping roof. He tilted it and filled a tin cup. He came back with it and handed it to Wheaton, who said, "Sir— I'd like to."

"Drink it, then."

Pvt. Wheaton turned and appealed silently to the sergeant.

The sergeant said, "Lieutenant, you know that the major ordered him not to get anythin' to drink till four?"

"I know," said the lieutenant, "but look at the man's lips." They were cracked, and through the cracks tiny trickles of blood slid down his dust-covered chin.

"Yeah, it's hard," agreed the sergeant. "But the major ordered it. It's a punishment, and like the major said, Wheaton won't die. I don't want to see you get into trouble, Lieutenant, and Wheaton here don't want to get into trouble for drinking it, and he don't want you to get into trouble, either. So, all in all, Lieutenant . . ."

"Sergeant," said the lieutenant, "I want you to get me another shirt from my room. The grey one'll be fine."

The sergeant looked mournful, "Yes, sir," he said.

"Take about five minutes," added the lieutenant.

As soon as the sergeant turned the corner the lieutenant held out the cup. Wheaton licked his lips. "Gee, Lieutenant," he said, "I don't think . . ."

"Take it."

"Lieutenant . . ."

"This is an order, Private Wheaton." Wheaton drank. Then he picked up his log and resumed his tour. The lieutenant replaced the cup and sat down on the bench, watching the dust clouds which meant parties of Indians were nearing the Fort. Most of them came from the northeast, where the heart of Comanche country lay.

"Afternoon, Stowe." Mr. Cross stood behind him. The lieutenant nodded. "How're things, Stowe?"

"Fine, Mr. Cross. And by the way, you will notice I call you 'Mr.' I have a rank. I want it used in front of my name."

Cross took his cigar out of his mouth, narrowed his eyes, tugged the lobe of his left ear with his fingers. His fingers were dirty, and the constant tugging at his ear had made the lobe filthy. He was thinking. Then he grunted, and said, "You're right, Lieutenant. You got a rank and I'll respect it."

It was evident that he needed someone to talk to and was willing to back down somewhat for an audience. Before he could get started Sgt. Christie came around the corner of the stable. He looked more depressed than ever as he saw Cross. By now, the lieutenant knew that was his way, frequently, of expressing deep pleasure. The sergeant stopped in front of Cross, and said, "I see you come up from the river all right."

"Why shouldn't I?" asked Cross, surprised.

"How are they?" asked the sergeant, leering.

"How are what?"

"You know, what you went down there to look at. Did you creep up real close through the elder bushes and have yourself a good time lookin'? Because I think that's all you do in that department, just look."

"That's enough, Sergeant," said the lieutenant. "It's four. Tell Wheaton; let him drink, and be sure the trumpeter sounds retreat."

He waited until the sergeant had left and Cross had wandered off, his face red with anger. Then he walked up to the Administration Building. Lt. Wynn was sitting at his desk and waving a fan. "Oh, my God, sit down, Stowe," he said. Lt. Stowe sat down. Lt. Wynn crossed his legs, and pulling the trousers delicately away from his skin, bent down and waved the fan at his ankles, trying to push the air up his legs.

"This is about all I do all day," he said, "till sundown. You want to see the major?" Lt. Stowe said he wanted to get orders for the next day.

"He's—er—resting," said Lt. Wynn. "Whenever he's resting, do whatever you want." Lt. Stowe nodded and turned to leave.

The door opened and Beth walked in. "Afternoon,"

she said. Lt. Stowe straightened and bowed. He did so awkwardly, and for some reason this pleased Beth. She smiled.

"I'm going swimming with Tall Woman," she said. "How's Dad?"

"He doesn't want to be disturbed," said Lt. Wynn.

"Oh," she said.

"Tall Woman?" asked Lt. Stowe.

"Tall Bear's daughter. We go swimming together all the time whenever she comes to the Fort. But I swim better than she does." She smiled and left.

"She does," said Lt. Wynn.

"She does what?"

"Swims better than what's-her-name. Sat once atop my horse on the bluff and I happened to look down at the river with my field glasses when I heard the girls laughing and I saw her in the water." He sighed. "She was naked."

Lt. Stowe felt a swift flush of anger. Lt. Wynn went on, "But I never did that again. I saw no point. No point at all in driving myself crazy." He unbuttoned another button on his shirt. "She likes you, though," he went on.

The lieutenant flushed. "She does," said Lt. Wynn. "She said this morning you had a face and not many muscles." He grinned.

Lt. Stowe said, "Well, I'll be going," feeling very pleased.

"Don't go yet," said Lt. Wynn, wistfully, indicating the pile of papers on his desk with a sweep of his fan. "Don't leave me alone with those!" He held the fan directly above his head and waved it downwards. "Here, let me read you a couple." He leafed through the pile. "Here," he said, grinning, "read these two requests for leave. One is mine, that's the first one. The other's Boo's."

The first one had written across it simply, "I told you twice, Goddammit! No!" The second was a request for a week's leave, and the Major had written on it, "Request granted, but cut down to 48 hours. That is as long as any reasonable man can wish to stay in bed with the same woman.''

Lt. Stowe said goodbye and walked down to the corral, where he found the sergeant and told him the plans for the next day's troop practice, which included having the men ride three hours without water.

"That sounds pretty rough, sir," said the sergeant.

"It ain't regulation," said the lieutenant, "but from what I hear of Texas, waterholes don't always appear on regulation." The sergeant nodded.

From behind the barracks Beth appeared with a tall Comanche girl. Their long thick black hair hung down their backs, wet and shining. Beth came up and said, "This is Tall Woman."

Tall Woman looked at Stowe; then she smiled and turned to Beth. She drew her forefinger along her forehead; then she drew circles in the air next to her right ear. She placed the forefinger and the second finger of the right hand astride her left index finger, and, finally, pointed to the sun. Then she smiled, and, drawing a comb from a small leather pouch she carried at her belt, began to comb her long hair.

"What did she say?" asked Stowe, fascinated.

"Well," said Beth, "the line along her forehead meant 'white man,' because only whites wear hats. Circles in the air meant the same as with us: 'crazy,' and the two fingers atop her index finger meant 'on horseback.' She meant you were all crazy to ride in this heat."

Tall Woman stopped combing and made more sign talk. Beth blushed.

"What did she say now?" Stowe asked.

"Well," said Beth, "you must understand Comanches are frank about—well—people. She said that since you are tall and I am tall you should buy me from my father and then we would have many tall sons. Then she said that you and I—"

"That's enough," said Stowe.

"I told her," said Beth, "that you did not have enough horses to buy me."

Tall Woman thrust out her open hand, made grabbing gestures, and pulled her closed hand towards herself.

"'Then steal them!'" translated Beth.

Lt. Stowe said, remembering the 3rd US brand on the horses of Yellow Bird's band, "Ask her how many wives does Yellow Bird have?"

The smile vanished from Tall Woman's face. "She says her heart is heavy, and that she cannot joke with you," said Beth. Tall Woman touched Beth's shoulder and walked away. They watched her go.

"If I said anything wrong," began the lieutenant.

"No, no," said Beth. "You didn't know. Yellow Bird leads many of the younger chiefs. Her father leads the older ones. Tall Woman is afraid Yellow Bird will pull the Comanches into war. She is afraid I will hate her because many of the soldiers will die. Every spring for three years now we have gone swimming together. She is afraid all this will end."

"Will you teach me sign talk?"

She nodded. "First lesson," she began.

She made a circle with her right thumb and forefinger. Then she moved her arm to the right and dropped it about a foot. "Sunset."

She placed her hands, palms down, before her face, and then they went up and out in a big curve and ended, palms up, at shoulder level. "Day."

Swiftly, she placed her right hand, palm down, over her heart, and moved it to her right. "Good."

"And 'good evening' to you, too," Lt. Stowe said. She waved, and the lieutenant watched her long stride until she was gone.

FOUR

At ten on Sunday morning the chiefs moved out from the shade of the cottonwoods and walked slowly to the Administration Building. Pease knew they would not be armed and he warned Major Welles of this. He had also told the major that the chiefs would probably discuss the treaty of Medicine Lodge. This was the four-year-old treaty under which they had come onto the reservation.

When the chiefs neared the porch the major saluted, as did his officers. Lt. Stowe stood several feet away from the major. Captains Mason and Drake were next to the major; Lt. Wynn stood between the captains and Lt. Stowe, and Pease stood between the officers and the chiefs, as if as a sign of his neutral status, since he was to be interpreter.

None of the officers were armed. The major was spotless, clean-shaven; he had slept well. Lt. Wynn whispered, "Looks good, eh? He hasn't touched the bottle today. I didn't hear that bottom drawer of his squeak all morning. He never touches it when big stuff is on. But on regular garrison duty—why, you remember the day you came? He was just back from . . ."

"Lieutenant Wynn! Have the courtesy, if not the intelligence, to be quiet." Major Welles turned to the chiefs and said, "Mr. Pease, will you be good enough to interpret?"

Pease turned to the chiefs and said a few words. Then Crazy Elk arose and spoke. He said, "Our horses are poor. It is warm weather and the horses have given out. All the streams are dry and there is little water; they sent us ahead to meet you. We have come and it is good to see you.

"This summer we were on the other side of the Cimarron, near the Big Snowy Mountains. We were getting skins for our lodges. In the fall traders will want our robes. We will then cross the Cimarron to Judith's Basin, and hunt.

"We do not shoot our white friends." The younger chiefs looked sour at this, but there were no interruptions, since this would be considered rudeness.

Lt. Wynn whispered, very quietly, so that Major Welles would not hear, "That remark was made for the younger chiefs. Pease is sure they are hot for raiding with Yellow Bird into Texas."

Crazy Elk continued. "We are true when we look you in the face. On Deer Mountain white men come. They are my friends; they marry Comanche women; they have children by them; the men talk Comanche. We raised Pease; he was a boy when he came here."

He sat down. Running Wolf rose. He said, "We do not want Pease to go away. My boy does not want Pease to go away."

From his pouch he took an elaborately carved wooden stick. "That's a pledge for a horse," whispered Lt. Wynn.

Running Wolf walked to Major Welles and held out the pledge stick. "My boy gives you a horse to keep Pease here," he said, and returned to his seat.

Two little girls came forward; each held a tanned buffalo robe. Pease stood between them, and placing a hand on one, said, "This is Tall Bear's youngest daughter, and this chubby one is Kicking Eagle's daughter."

The chubby little girl said, "We want Pease to stay with the Comanche tribe." They placed the robes carefully at the major's feet.

Pease tickled each girl, very gently, back of an ear, as they turned to go. The chiefs smiled, and then became serious as they watched the major stare at the pledge stick and at the robes. He spoke.

"Mr. Pease, tell them I know what is in their hearts. And say the Great White Father knows, also, what is in their hearts. But the Great White Father has many children and some of them need a good father like Pease more than others; more than the Comanches need him. The Great White Father sees everywhere, and knows more than we do who see only the prairie close to us."

Tall Bear said, "Did the Great White Father make the treaty at Medicine Lodge four years ago?"

"Yes."

"Then," said Tall Bear, "this is what we were told at Medicine Lodge. What we were told there we have in our hearts. They told us to look out for a white man with a good heart for our agent. We have found him. Here he is in Pease. He does not drink whiskey; he likes us. He does not offer us whiskey, and we like him. The children all like him."

"I have the treaty here," said Major Welles. He held it up. "You have put your mark on it, Running Wolf, and you too, Tall Bear. That means you approve of it. Nowhere in the treaty is there anything about Pease."

Running Wolf stood up. Lt. Stowe could see he was becoming angry, although it was considered poor etiquette to show emotion or to speak swiftly in council.

"We do not forget," he said. "That day at Medicine Lodge we asked that the white man's road along the Clear Fork of the Brazos be abandoned and that grass be permitted to grow in it. They said, 'yes, yes,' but it is not so in the treaty. We asked, 'Shall our children and ourselves get food for forty years?' They said, 'yes, yes,' but it is not so in the treaty. They told us when we got a good man for an agent he should stay with us, but it is not so in the treaty."

Major Welles said, "It is hard to tell you this, but the white man who told you these things should not have done so. They cannot stop the white man's road. No one can. Can you stop the Red River by putting your hand in it? Can you stop the whirlwind by shouting 'Stop'? No one can stop it. That day at Medicine Lodge . . ."

There was a murmur among the younger chiefs. Suddenly one stepped forward, and defying the shocked faces of the older men, said, "I am Black Beaver. I wish to speak. These are old men; we are just grown up. The Apache have stopped the white man's whirlwind. And who are the Apache? They have few horses! We once roamed from the Platte to Chihuahua!"

He waited. "It was not hard for the Apache to stop the white man's whirlwind." His voice was contemptuous as he repeated the phrase. "Are the Apache braver than us? Look, I have counted coup many times!" He signalled, and his woman stepped out and came forward, holding a buckskin-wrapped object. Black Beaver unwrapped it. He took out a war bonnet and held it high. Each feather meant an act of bravery in the face of the enemy, and the last brilliant feathers of the bonnet trailed on the dusty floor. "You old chiefs have war bonnets like this—some of you have counted more coups than I. Have you become women?" He paused; then he turned to the major. "There will be a tall man in the store named Cross. He makes bad faces to us; he is a hard man. We do not know him. He will be bad to us. And I am not a fool. In Texas the whites have no horses on the Pecos or on the Sweetwater, and over to Wild Horse Creek their horses are in the Cheyenne camp.

"I will now tell you about that treaty. It is all lies. We do not want to hear any more. Wrap it up and throw it away. We will not have that treaty. We sell our land, and what do we get for it? I am ashamed about it. We get a pair of stockings and when we put them on they go to pieces. They get some old shirts, and have them washed and give them to us; we put them on, and our elbows go right through them. Why should we take them? We did not put our names on the treaty. Who are these old men? Once they were great war chiefs. Now let them burn their war bonnets!''

He turned and walked through the chiefs and down the porch steps. Several of the younger chiefs followed him. The old chiefs sat for a moment, their hard brown hands resting quietly in their laps. They did not look at each other or at the major. They stared at their hands. Tall Bear's youngest daughter came up to him and put her hand through his elbow. He slowly rose, and spoke.

Pease said, ''He says thank you for the food and for the use of your meadows for his horses. He says the grass is very fine. He says you have a good heart. And that you talk straight.''

Major Welles said, ''Tell him it was good to talk to him. Tell him I hope we shall always be friends. And tell him that there shall always be a meadow here for his horses.''

Tall Bear said, ''There has been trouble on the line between us and i thought it was all over. But now my young men will dance the war dance. But it was not begun by us. It was you who sent out the first soldier and we who sent out the second. So it was upon the Brazos. When we found them we killed them and their scalps hang in our lodges. First there came Texans and made war. We took their road and went on it. The white woman cried and our women laughed. If they had kept out of my country there might have been peace.''

''I am sad to hear this talk,'' said Major Welles.

Tall Bear shook hands with his left hand, saying, ''I shake hands with this hand because my heart is on this side. I am sad too. I shall paint my face black and shave my pony's tail in grief for what will happen. The Texans have taken away the places where the grass grew the thickest. I thought that was all over. I see it is not."

He left. Tall Woman walked to Beth. Her right hand touched her own heart, then it went out, touched Beth's heart lightly, and came back to her own.

Then she followed her father to the Comanche camp.

FIVE

The next afternoon Lt. Stowe walked his favorite black mare, named Sassy Ann, up to the meadows, and turned her out to graze. Sgt. Christie was already there, squatting on his heels and talking to two corporals and Pvt. Wheaton. When they saw the lieutenant they started to rise. "At ease," he said. They squatted again, and made room for him. He went down, too.

The men went on drawing aimless circles with dried grass stems. One of the corporals began drawing "3rd US" again and again, brushing it out, and writing it again.

"How's the shoulder, Wheaton?"

"All right, sir. A bit sore. But that fifteen dollars— I'm gonna miss that next leave."

The corporal began drawing wavy lines. Then a bar underneath. He rubbed it out and then he tried a circle and a plus sign in the middle of that. Sgt. Christie laughed at the lieutenant's puzzled face. "Tell the lieutenant what you're doin', Schweizer," he said.

"Sure," said Cpl. Schweizer, affably. "When this

country belongs to me, Lieutenant, instead of to them Comanches, I'm getting me a ranch. And I want a brand no one can burn over easy." He began to trace another combination. "Clean out the buffalo so the bastards'll leave the grass for my cattle!" He grinned. "Lieutenant," he asked, "how many years do you think that'll take?"

"I don't know," said the lieutenant. He rose.

"Is the lieutenant sore?" asked Schweizer. "I'm sorry if the lieutenant's sore. I know the lieutenant likes Comanches." His voice began to rise and he stood up.

"Are you crazy?" asked the sergeant. "Shut up!"

"Shut up nothin'! I'm from Big Springs. Do you wanna know what them Comanches did to my people? I was twelve and I was swimming in the creek below the ranch when I heard them. I hid in the tall grass and I heard my mother and my sister screaming for half an hour after they killed my dad. Do you wanna know what them Comanches did, Indian-lover?" His voice began to tremble.

Sgt. Christie stood up, sighed, and slapped Cpl. Schweizer with his open palm in the stomach, quite hard. The corporal sat down, looking surprised and agonized. He held his stomach with both hands, fighting for breath. "Are you all right, Ira?" Boo asked. Ira nodded, gasping. He rolled over onto his back and placed a dirty palm over his face, shielding his eyes from the sun. "I'm sorry, Lieutenant," he said.

Lt. Stowe said, "Forget it."

He walked through the meadow, toward the river. He weaved through a clump of waist-high alder bushes, and came out upon the deserted Comanche encampment, then he wandered among the old campfires, kicking at the charred logs and the old buffalo bones. Seeing something familiar he bent down and picked it up. It was the pledge stick that Tall Bear had offered to the major. It had been broken in two.

Someone was coming. He turned and saw Beth. "I came down, too," she said. "I have no one to swim with anymore." She was wearing buckskin trousers fringed down the seam, moccasins, and a blue and white striped cotton blouse. A necklace of turquoise and a small hoop of silver starred with turquoise hanging from each ear completed her outfit.

"You like it?" she asked, stroking the necklace. He nodded. "Tall Woman gave it to me," she said. "It came from Mexico a hundred moons ago."

He nodded again.

"You looked depressed."

"I am," said the lieutenant. He held up the pledge stick.

"I know," she said, "I saw it too." He tossed it into the river and they watched till it floated out of sight.

"Come and sit among the sunflowers," she said. "I always sit there when I feel like this."

He followed her through the great sunflowers till she stopped in a small clearing. "Sit down, Lieutenant," she said. He did, but she remained standing, thrusting her hands in her pockets and looking back at the great flower heads that were massed above like a galaxy of brilliant orange suns. She broke a stalk and hauled down the tall stem. She pulled out the petals one by one.

He reached down and took the huge yellow plate that was left after the petals had been stripped and he held it under her chin "You are crazy about butter," he said.

"Lieutenant—"

"Beth, have you ever been in Cherry Valley?"

She knelt down beside him and placed her hands on his shoulders. "Tell me about it," she said.

"Well . . . ," he began.

"But some other time," she said.

The lieutenant kissed her very slowly. He knew it might be the most important kiss of his life or that it might mean nothing to him. He was willing to face the fact that it might mean nothing to her, either.

The overhang of the cottonwoods cut off the sun. Her face was in shadow, her eyes closed. He put a hand on her back and through her blouse he felt the firm muscles tense in response and press against his palm. Then she pulled him beside her, still kissing, on a mat of dead sunflowers. High up he was aware of the drone of a few bees, and far in the distance the clang-clang from the blacksmith's shop. Behind her black hair spilled over the yellow petals she had pulled apart. She broke her mouth away, trembling, and pulled back to look at him. Then she took off her necklace, and she unscrewed her earrings.

"Beth," he began.

She covered his mouth with her hand and smiled. "Time for talking later, Sam," she said.

He gently took her hand away. "Beth," he said, "I like you too much for a flirtation down here in the cotton-woods."

She looked puzzled. "Well?" she said.

He stood up and pulled her to her feet. "May I visit you tonight at your home?" he asked.

She rose easily, and brushing her pants, said, "You're much too civil, Lieutenant. You're much too much the correct man from the Point . . . Goodbye." She turned and started to walk away, putting her earrings back.

He called out after her: "May I see you tonight?"

She paused, and looked at him for a moment, putting in the other earring. "All right, then," she said. She smiled. "All right, then. Tonight, at seven." She turned once more and strode away. Her ankle tendons showed slim and taut as she walked over the dead sunflowers.

The lieutenant rose and brushed off his pants. He had known many women in the course of four years in the Union Army. There were the women near the first camp. There were the women who followed the Army on its march. And there were the women of the conquered, who were happy to have an affair with anyone, as long as he was young and properly male. And with these he had passed the time pleasantly. He began to walk down the trail, toward the meadow. He picked up a dead cotton-wood branch and he slashed idly at the sunflower stalks.

But this girl—he knew she was willing to be treated as casually as any of the camp followers. And this he did not want. He chopped viciously at a stalk and cut it cleanly. It trembled a bit at the top, slid sideward off its stem, and fell softly across the path. He stepped over it and came out into the meadow.

Cross had been examining some of the horses out on picket. Across the meadow Sgt. Christie was training a platoon to swing from a column of two into a line charge. He took a break just in time to watch Cross as he petted a big grey named Hammerhead. Sgt. Christie hoped that the grey would bite him. He watched, disappointed, as Cross, unharmed, walked over to the lieutenant and spoke to him, although he could not hear what they said.

Cross said, pleasantly enough, "Afternoon, Lieutenant."

The lieutenant nodded, and turned towards his quarters. Far away across the meadow he could see Beth walking. The agent said, "Cigar, Lieutenant?"

"No thanks," said the lieutenant.

Cross lit his. "Some of your horses ain't half bad, Lieutenant," he said. "Bigger'n them Indian ponies, anyway."

The lieutenant said, "Most of those Indian horses are bred from the Spanish stock; that's why they're smaller." Cross nodded.

He took off his hat and waved it at his face. "Saw the major's daughter come out of the thicket there," he said. He put his hat on and looked critically at his cigar. He rolled it tenderly between his fingers. "A very nice lookin' girl, that one." The lieutenant said nothing. "She come out puttin' on her necklace," he went on. "She looked a bit mad, too. And her Indian pants she wears all the time—they was dusty like she'd been rollin' a bit." He grinned.

"I know my place," said Cross. "The Agent at an Army post—who the hell's he? A poor relative. The Army wants to take away his job. So I don't fool around with them balls the officers have. I'm pretty much dirt. And I hope you won't take offense, Lieutenant, but so are you. No offense meant or intended, but lieutenants aren't even worth a dime a dozen. They aren't even worth a nickel a dozen, they're so common. And they make just about enough money to buy shoe polish. So I never fool around with the officers' families. And I'd like to warn you, Lieutenant, that the major isn't gonna like a plain ordinary lieutenant sniffing around his daughter, whether she's in heat or not." He looked after Beth, who was almost out of sight around the corner of the enlisted men's barracks.

"Yes, sir," he added, "even if she's willin'."

He looked at the lieutenant. He winked, in a man-to-man manner. "Eh?"

The lieutenant said slowly, "Mr. Cross, I'll have to ask you to apologize."

Cross looked surprised. "I didn't hear you right, Lieutenant," he said. "Did you say you wanted me to apologize?"

The lieutenant nodded. "And if I don't," said Cross, "are you gonna have a duel with me, like a regular Army feller?" He took out his cigar, looked at it. "I don't shoot good and I don't know how to swing a pig-sticker. You'd be takin' advantage of me terrible." He grinned. "You're still waitin' for me to apologize?"

The lieutenant nodded, his lips pressed together.

"Well, look, now, Lieutenant," Cross said, easily, "don't get foolish. I didn't say nothin' bad about the lady. I just said she might be a good . . ." He stopped. "I can see by your face you won't take no for an answer. So, if you wanna step back here in the thicket there I'll try and help you out." He took a last puff and tossed away the cigar.

They walked inside and when they reached the small clearing where Beth and the lieutenant had been, they stopped. Cross said, "Don't come at me, Junior. I got the weight and reach on you." The lieutenant knew that

Cross was right. it had to be fast or not at all. He put his hands on his hips and smiled.

As he had figured, Cross relaxed at the lieutenant's apparent lack of fight. Suddenly he dove at Cross's legs. As Cross went backward into the sunflowers, grunting as he fell, Lt. Stowe hit him in the solar plexus as hard as he could. A solid mass of muscle covered Cross's stomach. The lieutenant had time enough to be surprised at this before Cross's big fist hit him on the side of the jaw.

The blow dizzied him, and as he dropped his guard Cross pulled him to a sitting position and hit again. He was knocked flat, and as he rolled out of the way of the kick that he knew was coming, Cross swung a leg. It missed his back, and the lieutenant scrambled to his feet and feinted high.

As Cross blocked, the lieutenant swung at Cross's jaw as hard as he could. Cross ducked and was hit on the nose. He stepped back, felt his nose with both hands, and looked at the blood in anger. Then he walked at Lt. Stowe and swung as hard as he could. His forty-pound advantage drove his fist through the lieutenant's guard and clipped him on the side of the jaw. He went down, unconscious.

Cross wiped the blood from his nose. Then he raised his foot to kick. "Heard a noise, Mr. Cross." Boo stood there. He walked over. "Had a big day here, Mr. Cross, I see. You got forty pounds on the lieutenant." He rolled up his sleeves. "Better grab yourself a rest, Mr. Cross," he said. "We're gonna be busy a long time here." Cross waited, snuffling and wiping the blood away from his nose. Boo walked toward him, smiling.

Cross feinted low and hooked a left. Boo dived under both and his head hit Cross in the belly. His great weight knocked Cross down. Cross spun around on the small of his back and kicked at Boo's groin. He missed. Boo grabbed Cross by the shoulder, pulled him to a sitting position, feinted at his stomach, and as Cross covered himself, Boo broke his nose. Then he pulled Cross erect, dragged him throught the sunflowers, leaned him erect against a cottonwood trunk and viciously swung his elbow into Cross's mouth. Cross spit out two teeth.

"More?" asked Boo. Cross shook his head. "Why not more?" asked Boo. "You don't like to fight people as heavy as you?"

"I'll have you discharged!" said Cross, mumbling through the blood and looking at his teeth on the ground.

"I guess you can do that," said the sergeant, "since you're always tellin' me you got powerful friends in Washington. Since I'm gonna be discharged . . ."

He chopped with the edge of his palm at Cross's neck. Cross's eyes went dull, and he swayed and pitched forward.

The sergeant went down to the river, and filling his hat with water, brought it back and threw some onto the lieutenant's face. The lieutenant came to and looked up. "Well," he said ruefully, "here I make another try." He stood up, weakly, and saw Cross.

"He's sleeping," said the sergeant, "and slightly spoiled." He added, "How you feel, Lieutenant?"

"All right," said the lieutenant. He felt his jaw and winced. The sergeant slapped Cross till he came to. "And Mr. Cross, how about you?"

"I . . . ," began Cross.

"That's mighty interestin'," said the sergeant, solicitously. He turned and walked through the alder thicket till he reached the edge of the meadows. "Hey, Wheaton! Get the ambulance!"

"The what?"

"The ambulance, dammit! Johnny Apples here hurt himself." He came back and looked at Cross, who had dragged himself to a sitting position against the trunk of a cottonwood. He was leaning his head far back in an attempt to stop the bleeding.

"Mr. Cross," said Boo, "you can do two things. You can tell what happened. But if you do that sooner or later

me or someone is gonna get drunk on pass and go huntin'
for you serious-like. And waitin' ain't pleasant.

"Or you can be bad and make up a fib and say you
was climbin' this here cottonwood and you put your foot
on a little branch and it broke. You fell and that face
of yours hit another branch and got disarranged, and then
you fell some more. That's a good story, and I like it.
I really do like that story, but I ain't gonna force you
to tell it. You just tell any story you want." He felt his
head. "I got me a little headache where I hit you in the
belly. You sure are built strong, Mr. Cross."

Cross looked up at the sergeant. Then he wiped his
bloody mouth with his sleeve. He was still a bit dazed.
"Lieutenant," he mumbled, holding his head, "you don't
know yet who your friends are. But you'll learn, you'll
learn . . ." He felt his nose and winced.

Boo turned to the lieutenant. "What's he yappin'
about, Lieutenant?"

"He wants to be my friend," said the lieutenant, "but
he just doesn't know how."

Wheaton and Cpl. Schweizer came panting down the
path with a stretcher. They set it down, put Cross on it,
and lifted him. As they went back Wheaton asked,
"What happened, Sergeant?"

"Ask Mr. Cross."

"I fell," said Cross. "Out of a tree."

"What the hell were you doin' in a tree?" asked
Wheaton, astonished.

Cross was silent. "Mr. Cross has got himself a hobby,"
said the sergeant, "and he's shy about it. He collects
birds' eggs."

Wheaton's jaw dropped. "Yeah," went on the
sergeant, "and he told me he coulda swore he saw a blue
warbler's nest up there. So up he shot. What happened
then, Mr. Cross?"

"I put my foot on a rotten branch and it broke."

"Very good," said the sergeant, approving. He
followed the stretcher, whistling.

The next afternoon the sergeant stood in front of the Administration Building, watching the eight Indian ponies tied to the hitching post. Their ears were laid back and their nostrils flared nervously at the strange sights and sounds.

Lt. Wynn came out on the porch and saw the sergeant.

"Sergeant," he called. "See to it that the men and horses are fed."

"The men inside, Lieutenant?"

"Yes. They're Osage. They heard about the Comanches pulling out and they want to be scouts if trouble comes."

"If?"

"Make it 'when'." Lt. Wynn went back in. One of the Osage spoke some English. He was saying to Major Welles, "Seven dollar a week."

"Four," said the major. The Osage looked admiringly at Lt. Wynn's blond hair.

"Seven," said the Osage spokesman, stubbornly.

"Great White Father likes you, but he does not have many dollars."

"Seven!"

"Five, no more, plenty meat." The major rose.

The Osage made a face. "White meat bad."

"On business trip many buffalo," said the major. "And many scalps, plenty good horses."

"No—" began the Osage. Then the major cut him off. "When the Comanche first knew you, you had nothing but dogs and sleds. Now you have plenty of horses, and where did you get them? You stole them from Mexico."

The Osage stood astonished at the major's knowledge of this bit of Plains scandal—not that the horses were stolen, but that there was a time when they had only dogs. Then the major pressed home his advantage. "Many scalps, plenty horses, too."

"All right, six."

The Osage said it weakly. The major shook his head calmly. The Osage conferred among themselves a moment. Then the spokesman nodded. "All right, five."

"I'll go down with them," said the major. "Lt. Wynn, you play major while I'm gone." He stepped out on the porch with the Osages. "And, Sergeant, these Osage will bunk among your men."

The sergeant made a face. "They don't smell so good," he said.

"And make sure your men get to know them by sight and by name," the major said, unheeding. "I don't want any of them shot by mistake if they get mixed among Comanches in a skirmish."

"Yes, sir." The sergeant turned and muttered, "They'll know 'em by smell."

"And, Sergeant!"

"Yes, sir."

"It won't hurt to give your men a talk on the difference between Osage and Comanche war paint. The scouts will look different with all that muck smeared on their faces."

The sergeant nodded and walked away with the Osage, passing Lt. Stowe on the way. The major was too close for him to say anything, but he winked as he saw the large bruise on the lieutenant's jaw. The Osage did not attach much importance to red hair, so they paid no attention to the lieutenant.

The lieutenant saluted. Major Welles examined the bruise in silence. "I get the daily sick list from the surgeon," he said.

"Yes, sir."

"Black eyes, gunshot wounds, kicks from horses, and those afflicted with certain unfortunate diseases due to brief and impassioned dalliances."

"Yes, sir."

"There seems to be an epidemic among you birds' nest collectors." His voice was icy.

"Yes, sir."

The sergeant was back, having handed over the scouts to Cpl. Schweizer. He had heard the major's last statement, and his mouth spread in a large grin. "And between we three," continued the major, "I consider Agent Cross's appearance to be considerably improved." The warmth suddenly ended. "One more thing. I was watching yesterday's saber practice. There is entirely too much emphasis on the edge. Comanche shields can stop a swing easily. And if the edge does connect, about all you can hope for is a surface wound. And you can easily parry a cut with a lance or a bow.

"But as for the point—no one likes to see a point come full speed at him. Not even a warrior out looking to count coup. When a point connects you are out of action. A side cut has only the rider's weight behind it. A thrust has the weight of the horse driving it home. So a little more emphasis on the point in tomorrow's practice."

"Major," said the sergeant, "I'm tellin' you now, the men ain't gonna like the Osage among 'em."

"Tell your men three things," said the major. "These Osage will most likely save the men's lives many times over because they can spot Comanche sign before your men. Second, we're not running a young ladies' seminary on etiquette. And third, the first example of mistreatment of one of these scouts will be rewarded with two weeks' solitary, and the next example, three. This is called arithmetical progression, and I can play that game all year. That's all, Sergeant."

As they walked away the major watched Boo make sign for "swimming at daybreak," and the Osages' stubborn shaking of their heads. Then he said, "Lieutenant, you've been seeing Beth."

"Yes, sir."

"Apparently she was involved in the cottonwood affair."

The lieutenant was silent.

"Her mother married me on the frontier, when I was a young lieutenant. She shivered in winter and sweated in summer. She died of pneumonia in Montana when Beth was ten. I don't want her to go through that for herself." The lieutenant was still silent. "Do you?"

"No, sir."

"She has known very few men. She is still feeling her way. If I were you, I would not take anything she says too seriously. And her background—what's yours?"

"Sir?"

"What did your people do?"

"Farming."

"How many acres?"

"Three hundred, sir."

"How long were they there? Cherry Valley, wasn't it?"

"Yes, sir. Eighty or so years."

"My family lived near Huntsford. In Maryland. For two hundred and twenty years. We had thirty-five thousand acres. The war ruined us; the house, and it was a magnificent house, was burned by Morgan's Cavalry, during the raids up through the Shenandoah Valley, and all my mother saved was a lapful of silver spoons.

"That background doesn't mean anything much out here, but it assumes great importance back east. Some day you'll be assigned there. It may mean a serious shock for you. Her friends will not accept you. I am not being cruel, Lieutenant. Think it over—and if you can find any permanent basis for a marriage besides love—and remember, love dies—tell me. Good afternoon."

"Good afternoon, sir."

He watched the straight back of the major stride toward the Administration Building. He was surprised to find he did not hate the major. Now he remembered that there had been a certain coldness between himself and most of the other cadets at the Point. He had thought then it was because he had come up from the ranks, and now he was beginning to realize it probably had been because of his background. It had made for four years of loneliness and not being invited to their fine homes on the long summer vacations.

In his first year he ate with his knife and he spat on the dining-room floor. He blew his nose with his fingers, as he had done all his life, and as all his people had always done. Four years of severe criticism by upperclassmen had taken that out of him permanently, but he became suddenly aware that Beth might be shocked at the way his father and mother ate, at his mother's calloused hands, at her poor grammar.

He did not think she would be shocked, but it was important for him to realize that he did not know her, after all, and that she was probably lonely at Fort Brill and that he was the only officer of her age. He decided not to see her in the future.

He was standing and thinking when Sergeant Christie returned. "Lieutenant," he said, grieving, "them damn Osage won't take a bath."

"Oh, for Christ sake," said the lieutenant, "don't be a baby!"

He walked away. The sergeant stared at him. "Man," he said aloud to himself, "whatever did the major jump him for?"

Near the window of the major's office, Agent Cross arose painfully from a bench. "I know," he said to himself, grinning. And as he walked very slowly away, he was still grinning.

SIX

There was smoke to the northeast next morning. Someone had seen a glow of fire a little before sunrise, and after the sun had come up it turned to smoke. Two hours later there were two more columns of smoke burning under an easy north wind.

The major sat on the porch of the Administration Building, and watched. To his left were Capt. Mason and Joe Pease. It was seven; they were all freshly-shaven. Their shirts were open at the throat, as it promised to be another hot day.

Capt. Mason was in his late fifties; a thin little sardonic man who yawned frequently. He was due soon for retirement, and he made it a point to keep out of harm's way. He was quite frank about it. He was a professional soldier and he had uttered two sentences along Sherman's line of march that had become classics among cavalry officers. An old slave had run up to his horse, kissed the captain's hand, and said, "Thank you, thank you, for makin' us slaves free," and the captain had withdrawn his hand, wiped it on his pants, and said, "I don't fight to free slaves—I fight for forty-five dollars a month and the goddamned Union!" —and went on to win the Medal of Honor in a cavalry skirmish outside Shelby. During this campaign he had also the misfortune to acquire piles, and he used to say, "I have the heart of a cavalryman and the behind of a nursemaid."

Pease's face was bitter. For a moment more the three of them looked at the smoke. There was no wind for several thousand feet, but at eight thousand the north wind hit the vertical columns of smoke and out of them made a vast black umbrella held up by three black pillars.

"Captain Mason," said the major, "go take a look-see. Take Lieutenant Stowe and give him a taste. As many men as you want; the Osage scouts."

Capt. Mason left, digging in his pocket for the Colt key. This was the key to the chest he kept under his bed, always locked. In the chest were stored the Colt revolvers which were currency anywhere on the frontier. They were issued only for patrol, never for garrison duty: this was to prevent their being sold.

The two men on the porch watched the plunging and kicking of the horses being saddled and the troopers running and buckling on their sabers and checking their carbines. Capt. Mason came out and began to issue the Colts. Far across the parade ground they could hear Sgt. Christie yelling, "You damn fool! The blanket edges go to the left!" Then the trumpeter sounded "Boots and Saddles," and the major took the salute as the patrol rode out.

"It's begun," said Pease.

"I don't know," said the major, knowing Pease was right. "Maybe it's Yellow Bird kicking up some dust."

"No," said Pease, "there's more than just one party out. Come over and have breakfast."

The major re-entered his office. Lt. Wynn rose. "Lieutenant," said the major, buttoning his shirt and combing his hair, "see that double picket is placed about the horses tonight and every other night from now on.

No one leaves the Fort unless they have a pass signed by me, and if you see Beth leave to go down for a swim, tell her not to, and if she goes anyway, tell me right away.''

They walked over to Pease's little frame house. Pease's wife, Crane in the Sky, was singing very softly in Comanche. Crane in the Sky had her long black hair plaited down her back, and it was adorned with silver buckles.

"She is singing for you," said Pease.

Pease's daughter, Swift Otter, stared at the major. She was only four, and a fat black braid hung down in front of each shoulder. The major reached down and tried to get her on his lap, but she wriggled off and said, indignantly. "I'm a big girl!"

"Sometimes even big girls liked to sit on my lap," said the major, pretending regret.

She was not moved. She said firmly, "But I'm a *very* big girl."

"Oh," said Pease, "sit on the major's lap." But she wouldn't. She ate a biscuit and would have none of the major.

"She looks so serious, that one," said the major, "like a sergeant with an idea coming along." She squatted on the floor and hugged her horribly mangled blue-eyed doll that had once belonged to Beth.

"She's a lonely little thing," said the major. "I see her sitting alone on the bench outside all the time with that old doll Beth gave her. Why doesn't she play with the NCO's kids?"

"They won't let her," said Pease. "They call her 'dirty half-breed' and throw stones at her. Come here, Momma." She leaned against her father's knee and stared at the major. Pease pulled the buckskin off her shoulder. There was a dark bruise. "She fights back, but she's alone, and she's only four."

"She fights back, does she?" said the major, slowly. "You should be proud of her."

The major walked outside with Pease. "Joe," he said,

"what will she have in five, ten years? She's going to grow up into a very pretty girl. It won't get easier for her."

"I know damn well it won't."

"You have to take her east."

"I can't," said Pease. "This country is my life. And back there Crane in the Sky would die remembering green-up time." He turned abruptly and walked away.

The major shrugged and walked to his office. As he walked up the steps, Lt. Wynn came out and said, "The wagon train—"

"—is overdue," said the major. "I hope it's not out there, and if it is I'll send out a heavy patrol tomorrow to meet it."

He turned to take a last look at the patrol. High up on the eastern ridge the last troopers in the patrol were outlined against the sun for a second. Their buttons seemed to burst into tiny splinters of fire. Then they were gone.

SEVEN

The advance scout, an Osage named George Washington, halted and waited for the column to come up. Then he pointed to the ground. At the side of the road was a small pile of fresh shavings.

Capt. Mason nodded. "What is it, Captain?" asked Lt. Stowe.

"War party sat here making arrows," said the captain. The Osage clenched and unclenched his fists three times. "Thirty of 'em," added the captain.

Without any warning, a man rode out of a gully. He was in civilian clothes, wore a black beard, and had big black eyebrows. His eyes were black also, and his hair and his beard made a sort of cowl around his face. His skin was pale, his fingers were long and bony, and he rode in and out of boulders skillfully, with his hat in his hand. His horse was as black as himself. His eyes were round and enormous. "Good day," he said, in a deep bass, and when he opened his mouth they saw that his teeth were very white.

"I saw some Indians going by a little while ago," he said, calmly. "I hid out till you came along, gentlemen."

He was a missionary, he said, as he rode along with them. He had been sent out by some obscure Baptist sect back east, to inquire into the spiritual conditions of the soldiers. He had a habit of working his scalp halfway down to his eyes when he spoke, and when he smiled—though he never laughed aloud—his eyebrows did not contract, as did most people's, but expanded instead till his eyeballs stuck out of his head. Whenever he smiled, several of his white teeth were seen to be pointed and the rest had a jagged edge as if he ate stones, and his skin grew even paler. His name, he said, was Dimpdin.

"The Army has not even the form of Godliness," he said. "This is a calamitous fact. I would it were not so. I grieve to state it! But inquiry into the fact has satisfied me that the form of Godliness does not exist. Ah!"

The Osage stared at him, wide-eyed. "For example," said Dimpdin, "I made some remarks to the Sixth Cavalry a few weeks ago. The officers directed the men to attend; I opened divine service with a feeling hymn, a very feeling hymn! By Montgomery! I commenced earnestly in prayer. I spoke advisedly for a short hour. What were the results? There were men, sir, in that assembly, who went to sleep. To sleep!"

He went down to an even lower bass, and his scalp went down to the bridge of his nose. The Osage were very impressed.

"And there were men, sir, who did worse. Not simply failing to be hearers of the word! But doers of evil! Men who played cards during the services. Played cards! Gambled! And some 'abandoned wretches' who mocked me! Mockers, gamblers, slumberers!" The horses were nervous, but Dimpdin had finished, and he smiled like a window dummy.

They reached a small stream, and the missionary dismounted and produced a wicker-encased bottle. "Young men love stimulating drinks," he said. "Strong drinks! Alcoholic drinks! Here is a portion of Monongohela! Old Monongohela! We will refresh ourselves!"

"I'll be damned if he hasn't got a lemon!" said Capt. Mason, in reverence, as Dimpdin pulled it out with a flourish, brandished it triumphantly aloft, cut it in half with an enormous sheath knife, and added sugar with great dexterity. The officers and Sgt. Christie all took some, and he emptied the rest with an "Ah!" that seemed to reverberate from the low hills. He shook hands all around, but would not listen to appeals that he should ride with the patrol for safety. He cantered off.

"I'm going to hear his voice for weeks," said Lt. Stowe.

The great heat had brought out the rattlesnakes, which the Osage lanced with great glee.

They rode on. The sergeant swore at the heat. Lt. Stowe looked at him, and asked, "How'd you ever get into the Army?"

The sergeant smiled. "I was a kid hoein' corn and I had hayfever," he said. "All the tassels were ripe and the air was full of that yaller dust like a snowstorm and I come down the row hoein' and sneezin' and cursin' and the tears kept runnin' down my face and I looked up and there were nine million more rows and I just threw away that hoe and kept goin' and I went right into town and got a job in a blacksmith shop and a year later I heard a drum beatin' and a bugle blowin' and I thought I never heard anythin' so beautiful my whole life, so here I am."

He laughed ruefully. "And my first battle! I was lyin' on my belly under an oak right in the middle of summer and I heard a bee over me and I looked up to see where he was goin' because we didn't have no sugar and the idea of honey was mightly nice. And right in the middle of a big oak leaf I saw a big brand new hole. I started right then to wriggle out of there for safer parts and I went half a mile on my belly, humpin' and flattenin', humpin' and flattenin', like a caterpillar on a leaf, and in five minutes I was right back under that tree where it all started, firin' enthusiastic-like at them bluejays, what we called you northerners."

"How'd you get turned around, Sergeant?"

"Well, Lieutenant, I bumped right into one of our patrols, and when a man has half a dozen of them reckless and desprit troopers lammin' him along the road on a tight run, and wallopin' him with the flats of their sabers, he don't have no trouble turnin' around. But nobody said a word to my lieutenant, and I got through my first battle without any shame bein' made public, exceptin' I had to keep buyin' them five troopers whiskey until two of 'em got killed outside Vicksburg and a third deserted, and two got transferred to Longstreet's corps. . . . Those are buzzards up there, Lieutenant."

There were hundreds of them circling easily in their big open spirals. Below them was the Lawrence ranch. All that was left standing was the big stone chimney. The rest of the house was a mass of charred and smoking beams. Ten feet beyond the front door were the bodies of Mr. and Mrs. Lawrence and their six-year-old son. All had died of arrow wounds, and all had been scalped. Sgt. Christie told off a burial detail. The captain watched them unpack the shovels. "We may as well eat, Lieutenant," he said.

The rest of the patrol dismounted, fed the horses, and began to eat. The lieutenant had seen many dead men in his life, but never any that had been scalped. And he had never seen a dead woman. She had been a handsome woman in her middle thirties, and it was a shock to the lieutenant to realize that with her mouth open and the flies buzzing around the dried blood on the top of her head that she looked as ugly as any male corpse. The lieutenant had eaten on battlefields before, but he did not feel hungry. He was surprised to see that only a small bit of the scalp had been taken—a piece about the size of a silver dollar. In his ignorance he had always thought that the whole scalp was removed.

"Better eat, Lieutenant," said the sergeant, squatting down beside him. He was gnawing at a chicken leg. "We're gonna be in the saddle all afternoon."

After the burial party had finished and were eating their lunch, Capt. Mason said, "Suppose you try and tell me what happened here, Lieutenant."

"Well, sir, my guess is that they set fire to the house, and when the Lawrences came running out . . ."

The captain nodded, his mouth stuffed full of chicken sandwich. "She doesn't look raped," he said. "They must have been in a big hurry." He poured dust over his hands, rubbed them together to get the grease off, and said, "Let's go."

The patrol set off toward the second smoke. They got there two hours later. This was the Simpson Ranch, and a half a mile away they could see the buzzards lazily balancing on the north wind. As the captain and lieutenant waited for the burial detail to finish their work they walked their horses through the burned-up ground down to the creek that flowed nearby. It was dry as a bone, choked with ashes and dust, the cottonwoods on the banks afire. The trees on the other side had not been reached by the fire; they walked across and let the horses nibble at the tender shoots of the cottonwood. The creek had been completely dried up by the terrific heat of the fire, but in half an hour the pent-up water forced a passage through the ashes and the thirsty horses drank. The officers lay on their backs far up the other bank, away from the heat of the burning trees, and smoked.

Sgt. Christie came down to the creek and said, "All done, sir." He wiped his face with the bandanna he wore knotted around his neck.

"You got the crosses up?"

"Yes, sir."

Capt. Mason rolled over and stood up. "You know, Captain," said the sergeant, "I got a feelin' that everywhere we go today we'll be starting cemeteries."

The captain looked at him, then reached into his saddlebag and took out a bottle. "Take a big one," said the captain.

The sergeant did. "Thanks, Captain," he said, and

added, "Them Osage are gettin' restless."

"What's the matter?"

"Well, as near as I can make out, they don't want to hang around buryin' no one."

"I haven't asked them."

"I know, but they don't like this hangin' around anyways. They signed on to kill Comanches and they don't like this foolin' around with corpses. They say what good are corpses with the scalps gone? No good, they say. So let's us go and chase some Comanches, is the verdict. And right away."

Captain Mason was undisturbed at the news. "We have one more smoke to look at," he said. The sergeant nodded.

They rode eastward once more. The Osage scouts ranged ahead, two fanned out on each flank, and once in a while, as the prairie swelled up into gentle rises, the flankers loped a bit in order to keep pace with the patrol. Suddenly one of the flankers made the discovery sign. Pointing downward into a tree-lined ravine, he grinned, to show there was no danger. Capt. Mason relaxed. "Go on and take a look, Lieutenant," he said.

The lieutenant rode over. The two Osage had dismounted and one was poking his lance at what looked like an enormous dusty bee hive. He held his horse back when he saw it, but Sgt. Christie said, "That's a Comanche grave, Lieutenant. Safe enough if you ain't superstitious."

With their lances the Osage tumbled it to the ground; it was an old grave and the bones burst through the slits made by the lances in the cloth wrappings. The Osage were looking for valuables that the Comanches enclosed with the dead to accompany them to the Happy Hunting Ground. They got a fine bow out of this one, and further down the ravine they found another body in a tree: this one held a fine revolver.

Far ahead the Osage riding point suddenly began to gallop in a tight circle. Capt. Mason snapped, "Carbines out!"

The Osage began charging about on their hardy little ponies, putting them out of breath, so that when they regained their wind, they would not fail to sustain a whole day's battle.

Capt. Mason watched the flankers and rear scout for any sign of danger, as the point had given. Sgt. Christie was doing the same thing. They gave no warning, however, and the lieutenant watched the point again. The scouts had stopped their riding in circles and were waiting for the patrol to come up. When the patrol reached the scouts it halted. Capt. Mason looked down a broad slope. At the bottom a broad willow-lined creek was flowing along a sandy bottom, and past sand bars covered with low scrub. "Well," he said, "there's Wynn's wagons."

Sprawled across the shallow ford and on one bank were seven shattered wagons. The horses had their throats cut and had died struggling, in their harness. "I told you they're in a hurry," said the captain. "They're not even taking horses. Sergeant, gallop down fast with two men and see if anyone's left alive."

The rest of the patrol rode down more slowly, each man scanning the horizon for Comanche sign. It was obvious that the wagons had just started to ford the creek when the attack started. The Comanches had been hiding in the dense willow growth. The four-man cavalry escort, a sergeant and three troopers, and twelve teamsters, had grabbed their carbines, waded to a sand bar in the middle of the creek, and made their defense from there.

They had dug pits with their hands and six of them had died doing that. The rest had fought till their ammunition had given out: the pile of empty shells at the bottom of each of the pits proved that. Six more had died in the defense of the pits. All these were the lucky ones.

The rest had been taken alive and dragged to the wagons on the bank. Then the Comanches had smashed open barrels of kerosene and ripped open the sacks of corn. Blood and kerosene had swollen up the grains of corn, and the smell of that and of burned flesh was too much for one of the troopers; he dismounted hurriedly and was sick. Then he looked up, embarrassed, at the sergeant. No one said anything to him. He wiped his mouth, grateful.

One of the teamsters had been lashed, head downward, to a wagon wheel. He was spread-eagled and tied with rawhide. His arms and legs were feathered with arrows, but none were in his torso. When they had finished with that target practice, they had lit a fire under his head, and that was how he died.

As for the sergeant, gunpowder had been crammed into his mouth and touched off. His eyes were hanging down on his bare cheek bones, but in spite of that and his shattered jaw, he had managed to crawl in a circle a few times, screaming. The Comanches were amused for a while, then they drove a lance through his heart.

One of the scouts, who had ridden across the creek to follow a trail in the thorny underbrush and sharp stones left by the spring floods, rode back and said, "Me find soldier! You come quick!"

A hundred yards beyond the creek a private sat on some flat stones. His back was propped against the trunk of a dead willow tree that had been left there when the creek had changed its course fifty years ago. He was still alive. His hands were holding what seemed a mass of dirty pink and white snakes. When the officers were close they could see he was holding his intestines.

His lips were cracked from thirst. "Water," he said. The captain dismounted and took out his flask.

"Sir," said the lieutenant, "with that stomach . . ."

"I'm gonna die," said the private. "Gimme some good whiskey to die with."

The captain knelt and put the flask to the man's lips. His intestines were ripped and filthy. The Comanches had sliced open his stomach, pulled them out, and made him run. His back was full of gashes made by their lances where they had prodded him into running.

"They hid behind the willows," he said. "Maybe fifty. Their chief was Yellow Bird."

"How do you know?"

"I saw him at Medicine Lodge when they signed the treaty. It was him all right."

The captain pulled out his notebook, and wrote: "Yellow Bird led the war party that killed twelve teamsters and four men of the Sixth Cavalry at the ford of Sandy Creek, August 27, 1873. I was a member of the escort." The captain read it aloud and said, "Will you sign this?"

The man nodded and signed with a bloody hand. The lieutenant was fascinated with the care he took not to let his intestines drop. Sgt. Christie and the lieutenant signed as witnesses. The man moaned and bent over, rocking from side to side. Captain Mason wrote at the top of the paper the words, "Dying Statement."

"Listen," said the private. "My wife . . . write that I . . ." He died.

They buried the private on top of a little mound.

The captain turned to the sandy graves, and said swiftly, "The Lord is my Shepherd, He maketh me to lie down in green pastures. And I commit these bodies to the earth in hope of resurrection thereof. Let's go, I want to be back before sundown."

They had traveled half a mile when shots rang on the right flank. Capt. Mason half stood in his stirrups, yelled, "Follow me!"

The patrol went behind him, across the broken country, and a few minutes later they met two Osage scouts. One was severely wounded in his right side. Both of them cried out, "Comanche! Comanche!" The scouts had stumbled across the rear guard. In ten minutes, by pushing their tired horses, the troopers saw a few Indians on a distant ridge; they sent a few derisive shots at the cavalry, and started to outdistance them.

Capt. Mason rose in his stirrups and yelled at his men to chase the Indians. They spurred their horses as much as they could, firing as they rode, and one of the Indians' horses suddenly rolled over; he had stepped in a prairie-dog hole. He sent his rider sprawling. They could see the rider trying to pull the horse erect and mount him, but he slid off again and mounted another horse. "Broke his leg," said the sergeant, stopping to fire his carbine. The shot broke the leg of the new horse.

That angered the Indians and they turned and fired several shots; one of the horses was grazed across the withers, and Lt. Stowe felt something like a hand twitching at his sleeve. He looked down and saw the tear where the bullet had gone through.

The guns of the patrol carried further and had more impact. One of the men's shots hit a warrior in the back. They saw him bend over and lie close to the pommel of his pony. Another warrior rode up and grabbed the reins and cantered off, holding his friend in place on the saddle. They slowly began to outdistance the patrol and were finally out of rifle range.

Capt. Mason held up his hand. "All right," he said. "No use. Back to the road." They killed the horses with the broken legs and rode back to where they had left the wounded Osage scout with two of his friends.

Then the wounded Osage died. They dug a grave for him on the trail, and Captain Mason ordered a volley for him. The noise of the volley brought several Osage up on the gallop from the ridge ahead, where they were look-ing for Comanche sign; they thought the Comanche had circled back of them and were attacking the patrol. They galloped up to the side of the grave, and they sat there, motionless, on the ponies, feathers nodding in the breeze, and their lances gleaming in the sun. After the entire patrol had marched over the grave to prevent the Com-anche from finding it and digging up the dead warrior for his scalp, Capt. Mason mounted and gave the order to ride back to Fort Brill.

"Captain," said the sergeant, "I think you're gonna have to talk to the Osage first. They say they came a long way to Fort Brill. They say they are going back poor. Can't get Comanche horses; can't kill Comanche."

Each of the Osage had been squatting; each held a small piece of mirror in his left hand, and in the palm was a puddle of saliva which they kept renewing from time to time. Red, green, yellow and black paint was being applied in great streaks. "They're getting ready to play now, like you promised," said the sergeant.

The captain said, wearily, to George Washington, "You won't get your money if you leave. We're going back to the Fort."

"Fort Brill? Now?" said George Washington. The Captain nodded. George Washington became too furious to remember his few words of English. He broke into sign talk. When he had finished, Sgt. Christie said, "He says you speak with a forked tongue. He says you promised scalps and horses. He says now that they have a chance for them you are scared of the Comanches. He says all the troops are good for is to bury people. He says the Army is commanded by women. He says . . ."

"That's enough," said the captain. "Tell him we don't have enough food or ammunition with us for more than a couple of skirmishes. Certainly not for a two or three day running fight. Tell him that."

Sgt. Christie began making sign. Lt. Stowe could recognize some: a palm arched high in the air was the sign for chief; a hand placed over the heart and forearm moved to the right in a wave motion meant the Comanche, or the Snake People, since they moved as quietly as a snake.

While he was talking sign the rest of the Osage began to braid bits of red flannel into their horses' manes. When the sergeant had finished translating George Washington said in English, "Goodbye, Mason. I go now." He led the scouts to the northward, following the Comanche trail.

Captain Mason stared after them, furious. Then he shrugged. "Let's go back," he said.

The sergeant yelled, "Stand to horse! Mount! Forward!" The patrol headed back.

"It's times like this," said the captain gloomily, "when I'm sure I'll never get out of Texas alive. The heat, the damn scouts, the bad water. And the high price of good bottom land. Do you know what they want for just one acre?" He began to quote prices. The lieutenant was pretending to listen, and little by little he let Sassy Ann drop back. After a few minutes the captain stopped talking.

Sgt. Christie rode his horse up from the rear, and said quietly, "It's been quiet a couple of years. The major's got to feel his way, careful-like." The lieutenant nodded, but the sergeant caught the lieutenant's irritated look toward the captain.

"All right. Now let me tell you somethin', Lieutenant. Them Comanches breed the finest short-distance racers in the country, Kentucky included. They ride 'em in action. When they're comin' down for a raid or when they're goin' back they ride the worst ones they got.

"Now, each of them warriors brings along five or seven, or maybe even ten of his horses. Some of them own as many as a hundred. They got kids, fifteen years old or so, riding with the herds, and whenever a warrior wants a fresh pony he signals the kid, who cuts out the pony wanted, rides it over to the party, and rides back the worn pony. So they're always ridin' a fresh pony.

"Now, when we get news of a war party at least five, six hours have passed. By the time we get goin' another hour passes. And there they are, six hours ahead of us, ridin' fresh ponies all the way. And they ride a hundred miles without a stop if they figure they're bein' followed. They don't even stop to eat. How we goin' to catch up? But these Osage are so crazy for scalps they'll ride their ponies till their hearts burst. The captain's right, Lieutenant."

The lieutenant said, "Why don't we follow with our own herd?"

"I'll tell you, Lieutenant. Because that's a new idea. And you know how the army is with new ideas. They shy away from 'em like a hoss from a rattler. And suppose we do as you say. We have fresh horses? So have they. And they're still seven hours ahead. And suppose we catch 'em. This is a big suppose. All that happens then is that they scatter. And I don't know how to catch a Comanche in broken country. And if his pony drops, he fights afoot. And if you think that's easy, Lieutenant— I don't know what to do, Lieutenant, and neither does Captain Mason. We only hope we'll run into 'em by accident. Only he's smart. He ain't lettin' himself get hysterical about it.''

"Sergeant!" called the captain. "Put out scouts."

The sergeant dropped back and appointed a point and flankers. He made Wheaton the point. "And remember, Wheaton, for Christ's sake, every time you get near a possible ambush, look twice as hard. If they're gonna jump us, they're gonna let you through, so don't go off dreaming about San Anselmo.''

"I hear they got a new fancy house in San Anselmo," said Wheaton.

"Who told you?" asked the sergeant, interested.

"Some trader going to Santa Fe. He said they got a woman there over six feet tall. They call her the Great Western. They got faro, monte and chuckaluck. They got two new saloons . . .''

The patrol rode on. They filled their canteens twice along the way, and emptied them. About six they reached the road that led to the Anson Ranch. Two silver spoons lay in the dust among a mass of hoof marks.

The captain said, "Lieutenant, I think you better take another look.''

The lieutenant turned and rode hard. The sergeant dismounted and picked up the spoons. "How old do you make the trail?" asked the captain. The sergeant kicked at the hoof marks. "Six, seven hours," he said.

"Listen, Sergeant, the lieutenant liked Mrs. Anson, didn't he?''

"He only seen her once, but I'm pretty sure he did.''

"I think you better go and take five troopers. And, here," he reached in his saddle bag. "I found this." He handed the sergeant an old Bible. "I'll wait for you here."

The sergeant found the lieutenant standing over the body of Mrs. Anson. She had been shot in the throat. As she fell to her knees she had tried to break the shaft, and another arrow had pinned her left hand to her left breast. She fell on her face, and the force of the fall had broken the shafts of both arrows.

She had been scalped. The lieutenant turned her over. Her mouth was full of dirt. The house had been looted. Her three carbines were gone. The yard was filled with feathers from a ripped mattress. She had died trying to reach for the carbine which she had let drop when the first arrow hit her.

The sergeant had walked around the house; he came back and said, "Lieutenant, one of 'em strangled a chicken and she must've thought a coyote was at them. She came running out to shoot it."

The lieutenant said nothing. The five troopers rode up. They dismounted and asked where to dig. He looked around. There were no trees anywhere. "On the north side," he said. "Give her shade."

One of the troopers handed him the small Bible.

The lieutenant tied his horse to the porch rail, and as men dug the grave, he read slowly. He found the Twenty-third, and when she had been lowered into the grave, he read the whole Psalm.

EIGHT

"They're too far north of the buffalo," said Major Welles. "And so the war parties are beginning to drift south." The officers of Fort Brill were sitting around the big round mahogany table that stood in the center of the major's dining room.

"I am dissatisfied with the way the whole business was handled," said the major.

Capt. Mason took his hand down from his eyes and stared at the major. "No criticism of you, Tom," said the major. "It's the whole business of waiting for a fire to break out somewhere, then running to put it out, then running back and waiting for another fire to start, and so on. What does it all add up to? To this: the Third Cavalry have become expert undertakers." Capt. Mason put his hand up and shielded his eyes once more from the bright glare of the kerosene lamp on the table. The major said, "This is not the function of cavalry. We are almost totally ineffective. The scouts desert us, and I have no doubt word will reach the Comanches. And this report of our timidity will certainly increase the scope of their next raids. You know what their raids are like. I have found most Army officers have a tendency to charge the Comanches with cowardice because they do not read or practice the United States Army Regulations." He smiled. "Lt. Stowe . . ."

"Yes, sir?"

"This full moon—do you know what they call it in Texas?"

The lieutenant shook his head. "They call it a 'Comanche moon'," the major said. "Listen carefully, please.

"The raiders leave their home ranges during the dark of the first quarter of the moon. They hide somewhere— in a break, in a box canyon, in a small hidden valley— until the night before the full moon. Then they slip by the Fort, raid, and return to the north until it's time to raid again.

"Next time they try that we're going to jump them. We'll stand a good chance of surprising them, what with the Osage reporting our refusing to follow today. They'll probably be overconfident. Here's what we'll do: half of this post will be sent out on the fourth day of each new moon. They will scout vigorously, looking for these hiding places day and night, until the twentieth day of the moon. Then they will return to the post and will be relieved by the other half of the post on the next fourth day. Any suggestions? Criticisms? No? All right."

The officers were staring at one another. "This will mean we shall have a good chance of stumbling across a war party who won't be expecting us. If we do jump a party, and if survivors get back (it won't hurt to let a couple go), the knowledge that we're there, roaming around looking for trouble, should be somewhat of a deterrent for the next moon. Anyone have anything to say?"

No one had.

"And this way we'll take the initiative. We'll take it this time and we'll keep it. We'll keep whittling away at them with our ambushes. We'll soften them up. We'll cut away at their men, and they can't afford to waste any. We'll soften them up so that the odds will be heavily in our favor for a successful winter mop-up campaign. And if this plan doesn't work, I'll think of something else. Dismissed, gentlemen.''

The officers rose. Lt. Stowe walked onto the porch and watched the others walk away, their cigarettes glowing in the warm soft darkness.

He leaned against the rail. Suddenly he felt the porch boards give way slightly. He knew Beth was there. She always wore moccasins.

"You've been busy?"

He nodded. "I've missed talking to you," she added. "How's your jaw?"

"My what?" he asked. He had completely forgotten his fight with Cross. "Oh, that. It's fine."

"Let me see," she said, and touched his jaw with her fingers. He made no move to touch her hand. She took it away. "I heard about Mrs. Anson," she said. "After my mother died she helped me make my first grown-up dress. She used to hitch up a small buckboard and come down to the Fort with a carbine resting across her knees, and she would sew for hours."

"She was nice to me," said the lieutenant.

"Boo says you read the whole Twenty-third over her."

Down by the enlisted men's barracks the trumpeter sounded tattoo. "Well, Beth," he said. "It'll be 'Lights Out' soon. I'm tired. Good night."

"Stay and watch the moon," she said.

The moon was full and open as a great yellow rose and he knew she wanted him to kiss her. "Don't play with me," he said. He walked down the porch steps and across the parade ground.

She stared after him. Behind her the door opened and in the glow from the lamp Major Welles stood silhouetted. "Best come in, Beth," he said.

She leaned against the rail and said nothing. The major came out and stood beside her, smoking. "Maybe you had better go east," he said. "It's time you met people of your own age; I think it would do you good to visit your aunt in Washington. Your cousins would love to show you around."

She shook her head. "You can't stay out here forever," he went on. "You're twenty-four. Plenty of nice young men in Washington. It's time you got off the frontier. I don't want you to do anything foolish because you're lonely. And if you do go you can take Crane in the Sky and Swift Otter with you. It's going to be bad for them this winter. Joe says they won't go but I think I can persuade him to send them." She shook her head. "Think it over, Beth. Good night."

"Good night," she said. She heard laughter from the barracks. The trumpeter sounded lights out; slowly the lights began to go out, one by one. The major blew out the light on his big mahogany table, and all that was left was the moon. It was enormous.

Far to the north, Beth knew, the raiding parties were coming in and performing scalp dances. A few squaws would be gashing their legs and cutting their hair in grief because of the deaths of sons and husbands in the war parties, but most of the sounds would be of rejoicing. And tomorrow some squaw would begin to pound Mrs. Anson's silver spoons into buckles for her long hair.

NINE

The sergeant reined in. "Lieutenant," he said, "I don't think it's any use. I haven't seen a sign of antelope or buffalo. If we could scout westward another day or so . . ."

"My orders are no extensive scouting to the west," said Lt. Stowe.

"Well, it's Army bacon or nothin' then," gloomily said the sergeant. He hooked one leg over the saddle horn and added, "Besides, a shot would wake up the whole damned county."

The lieutenant nodded, and gave Sassy Ann enough rein to munch at the short grass. They were in the twelfth day of Major Welles's plan: ". . . to scout vigorously from the dark of the first quarter of the moon . . ."

Sgt. Christie said, "Ain't no such thing as a law in dealin' with Comanche sign, lieutenant, but it all boils down to this: when you see Comanche sign, be careful—and when you don't see any, be more careful. Besides, there's good grass and water around here, so there's a good chance they'll show up."

They began to work their way back, avoiding all the ridges wherever possible, because of the silhouettes they would make against the horizon. As they rode along one of the small valleys the sergeant asked, "Lieutenant, you thinkin' of gettin' married?"

"What gives you that idea?" he said, somewhat short.

"Just thought you might."

"I'm not."

The sergeant sighed. "I was married once," he said, and waited.

"Go ahead, Sergeant," said the lieutenant. "Tell me about it."

"I will, Lieutenant. Seems we was gettin' along, not wonderful, but gettin' along. Then everything seemed to get worse. Maybe my fault, maybe hers. Anyway, things was crummy. And then she says, all of a sudden, 'If you don't like me, give me a divorce and a half of what you got and I'll leave you.'

" 'Nuf said,' " I said, " 'and here goes.'

"I had two hundred and twenty dollars in cash. I gave her a hundred. I'll tell you later what I did with the other twenty. Then I went into the closet and took all my trousers and ripped 'em in half, and threw one leg on my side of the room and one leg on her side. I did that with all my clothes. Then I broke the cook stove to bits with my sledge hammer and gave her half of that. She had her head out the window by this time yappin' her head off, so I threw her in the closet until I was finished. Then I set to work sawin' the tables and chairs in half and breakin' the mirror to bits and weighin' out her half on the scales. When I was all done I took her by the arm, drove her to town, waited two hours for the train, bought a ticket by tellin' the man I wanted twenty dollars' worth goin' east because I was goin' west, and I put her on the train with the pant legs and the sawed-up chairs and the busted mirror. And do you know, from the time I put her in the closet till she got on the train she didn't say a goddam word?"

"If there's a moral there for me," said the lieutenant, "forget it."

"Yes, sir," said the sergeant. They halted at the foot of a ridge and crawled up together to the top. The sergeant pulled out his field glasses. He always tried to have the sun over his shoulder, but if this was impossible, he always shaded the lens with his hat or hand to make sure the sun would not flash off the lens.

Far off, against the sun, they could see streamers of dust. "Better not use glasses," warned the sergeant. "They'd flash like mirrors." The war party was following a trail which would take them four hundred yards away.

As they approached the lieutenant could see that the great cloud of dust rising behind the party was made by captured horses. There were at least three hundred. The body of the war party rode in front of the herd to escape the dust. There were about sixty warriors. From each of their long lances dangled one or two scalps. In the center of the party rode four white prisoners: three young women and a boy of seven. Their arms were bound behind them.

The two warriors riding advance scout had tied red silk ribbons into their horses' manes. When the party reached the crest of a ridge and saw a pool of clear water at the bottom, one of the jubilant riders yelled and spurred his horse into a hard gallop for the water. He had tied another red ribbon, ten feet long, to the tail of his horse, and it whipped and fluttered behind him in a brilliant thin slash of crimson.

The patrol slid down the slope and walked their horses till they would be out of sight when the Comanches posted lookouts on the ridges. Then they sat and waited till dark, because their dust would be easily spotted.

As soon as it was full dark they headed back. Two hours of hard riding brought them near the Comanche camp. The lieutenant held up his hand. The patrol stopped, and Lt. Stowe called over the corporals and gave his orders.

"We'll circle around them on foot," he said. "I'll allow half an hour for each man to get into place. The signal to shoot will be two quick shots from me. Be careful: they have prisoners. They'll probably be close to the fire. Right, Sergeant?" Sgt. Christie nodded. "I want two men to stay behind with the horses. No talking. Let's go."

Five minutes later one of the men, clinging to a small bush as he crawled up a slope, pulled it out by the roots, and the fall he took against a rock made his rifle clatter. There was no possibility remaining of a surprise attack after that, and the lieutenant fired twice into the air. Those few soldiers who were already in position began firing.

The Comanches ran for their horses. Some of them began firing up the slopes at the flashes of the rifles, while the four Comanche lookouts fired along the ridges at the patrol. The crash of the carbines and the rapid ringing discharges of the Winchesters terrified the captured horses, and when they broke in a stampede the only way that was open to them was through the camp. By this time most of the Comanches were mounted and kicking their horses up the slope to get out of the way of the herd. A few remained in the camp, yelling and firing at the horses, trying to turn them back.

But their effort was not enough. The horses ran over the fires and the bound prisoners, and the fires went out to the sound of screaming. Two of the Comanches had seized their prisoners and had placed them across their horses' withers, and they rode off to the north with them, after the fleeing horses.

Several other Comanches gained the top of the slopes, and from there fired down hill at the patrol, mercilessly lit by the moon. The patrol could find no good cover. They did their best, firing at the concealed rifles, but the disadvantage was too great, and when five Comanches had crawled around to the rear of the patrol and started firing up the slope at them, catching the men between two fires on the exposed hillside in the full moon, Lt. Stowe gave the order to withdraw.

The men pulled back, firing and harassed by the Comanches. One by one, the Comanches slid down the slopes to the camp and mounted their ponies, which were being held for them by the younger boys. As they raced off one of them noticed that one of the prisoners was still alive, even though the horses had gone over her. He spun his pony and drove his lance through her throat. Then he galloped after the others.

The patrol in pursuit found the same story all over again: the Indian ponies were fresh, and the riders kept changing horses as soon as the ones they were riding showed the slightest sign of fatigue. The patrol was outdistanced, but when they came back five hours later they had retaken eighty of the captured horses, most of which had been taken from Mexico, although there were several with Texan brands.

They buried the dead: six men of the patrol, the dead captives, and four dead Comanches. There were several wounded Comanches, as they could tell by the bloodstains they had found on the trail. Several of the troopers were wounded. One of them was shot in the stomach. He felt very little pain, but these wounds usually became infected, and then there was nothing they could do.

"Pour in the whole bottle of carbolic acid and pray," said Sgt. Christie.

It had been a good evening's work, all in all. They had inflicted some serious damage on the Comanches, taken almost a third of their horses, and might make them think twice about raiding that way again.

Late next afternoon the patrol sat by the cooking fires, smelling the acrid fumes of dried buffalo chips that were used to cook coffee and bacon. The dried dung was burning well, with very little smoke. Pvt. Wheaton strolled up. "Sergeant, have you tasted the bacon lately?"

"Yeah."

"And the coffee?" Again the sergeant nodded.

"Yeah," said Sgt. Christie, "war sure is hell. We didn't see any buffalo either. I don't like bacon flavored with

manure much, but then you're a soldier of the republic."
He scooped up a mouthful of beans and swallowed.
"This here is luxury for you, Wheaton. All you been used
to eatin' back home was some 'sweet 'taters and a small
chance of corn; nary vittles else.' That's the way they talk
along the Blue Ridge, Lieutenant."

Wheaton said, "No, it ain't. It ain't that way at all.
First place we don't come from along the Ridge. We come
further along toward Knoxville. . . . "

The lieutenant rose and kicked out the fire. "I'll take
tonight's scout," he said. "Sergeant, put a heavier picket
on the ridge tonight. The war parties seem to be heading
back; no loud talking. We'll take fifteen men with us,
Sergeant. I'll go take an hour's nap, and we'll start an
hour after sundown." He walked away.

"He's comin' along," said the sergeant. "Give 'im
another three years and he might make a good officer."

The half moon of late October gave them enough light
for riding. An hour and a half passed. Then the lieutenant decided to turn back. "Wheaton," he ordered,
"take a long last look from that ridge."

The rest of the patrol waited below. As Wheaton rode
up the slope, Sgt. Christie said, "You never been in San
Anselmo, have you, Lieutenant?" The lieutenant shook
his head.

"That's a hard place," said the sergeant. "They got
about a killin' a day there. Them cowpunchers comin'
off the range got to blow steam, and they all stick together
when the Third US hits town. The sheriff locks the jail
with himself in it and what with the boys from the XIK
and the Rio Hondo ranches in on payday shootin' out
all the town's lights and the Third all choked up with the
dust of these long patrols, why, there's excitement in San
Anselmo." He sighed, and a faint smile of pleasurable
anticipation crossed his face. "I'd like to show you San
Anselmo, Lieutenant, next time you might have the desire
to go see life in the big city."

Wheaton came riding hard down the slope. "I see what looks like a campfire," he said. "South a ways."

The lieutenant and the sergeant rode up for a look. "It's a campfire, all right," said the lieutenant. "Let's go over for a closer look."

They rode toward the red glow. When they were a quarter of a mile away, they halted. They walked the rest of the way, leaving the patrol behind; the last two hundred yards they crawled. At the top of the ridge above the hollow in which the fire was burning was a clump of mesquite. They wriggled through it and poked their heads through. Fifty feet below was a Comanche camp. Eight warriors were sleeping in their buffalo robes. Three others were sitting around the fire, talking and laughing loudly. They had killed an antelope that afternoon and were eating broiled ribs. Scattered among their legs and about the fire were empty and half-empty bottles of whiskey. One of the warriors raised his arm for a drink; the robe slid off one brown shoulder and when the arm came down the lieutenant recognized the flat face and jutting sharp nose of Yellow Bird. Near the fire a lance had been jammed into the ground and in the light from the fire the lieutenant could see four bloody scalps hanging from it. Two of them had the short blonde hair of very young children. At the other end of the hollow, two hundred feet away, thirty ponies cropped the buffalo grass. The lieutenant tugged at Sgt. Christie's arm.

The two crawled away until they could safely walk back.

"All right," said the lieutenant. "Here's the plan. Kill the ones asleep with the first volley. The other three we'll take prisoner. That lance in front of Yellow Bird—if he starts to use it you and I will shoot him in the leg. Nowhere else. That clear?"

"Yes, sir."

"You'd better post Schweizer away from Yellow Bird. We'll get as close as we can; every man will pick a target, and the signal to fire will be my shot. We'll walk the last mile—I don't want the ponies neighing at one another. Post two men with the horses and check everyone's carbines and ammunition."

They rode hard to the camp. In five minutes the men were mounted and riding back. Some of them grumbled at the speed, but the sergeant called, "Silence back there!" and it became quiet. He said to the lieutenant, "Shake 'em up a little. Do 'em good; they're sleepy." They pounded along in the half moon. From the patrol came the sound of creaking leather, the faint jingle of metal against metal, and the slap of the canteens against leather. A mile from the Comanche camp they halted.

The lieutenant said, "Take off your canteens and all your other gear. Just take your Colts, carbines, and ammunition. I don't want any talking. From here we walk. When we get close, shoot at the middle of their robes and keep firing till they stop moving. The signal to fire will be a shot from me. And for Christ sake— don't drop anything." The men quietly began stripping off their excess gear. "All right," said the sergeant. The men began to circle around the fire. The only dangerous part of the maneuver was that the Indian horses might become terrified and give the alarm. But the horses had been ridden hard, and had found such good grass and water that they were absorbed in eating and calmly accepted the sight and sound of men crawling near them.

The lieutenant fired his carbine into a robe-wrapped figure. The volley of the patrol followed so closely it sounded like an echo. Three of the robes did not move any more.

A few robes stirred, were pushed aside, and the Comanches rose. Several of them managed to grab a carbine or a lance but a second volley brought most of them down to their knees, or crumpled them into sitting positions. A third volley crashed and finished them. One warrior kept pumping his carbine, but he got weaker and weaker. The shots went higher and higher, until his last went straight up into the air.

Yellow Bird grabbed his carbine and began firing at the flashes of the patrol's guns. His shots went wide and suddenly he grunted and pitched forward. Sgt. Christie had come from behind, and, swinging his carbine by the butt, had caught him back of the ear. By this time another brave next to Yellow Bird had managed to stand, fit an arrow to his bow, and raise it. Christie swung his carbine once more. The warrior went down across Yellow Bird. The third warrior had been asleep with a revolver belt strapped around his fat stomach. He sat up, pulled a Colt, and the lieutenant shot him in the stomach. He looked tremendously surprised. Then he went to his knees and pitched forward across the fire.

The men arose and advanced warily. The lieutenant smelled buring flesh. "Pull him off," he said. Someone pulled the Indian off the fire. The sergeant found some chunks of mesquite wood and threw them on the scattered embers; in a few moments they were blazing brightly.

"Drag 'em all to the fire," the lieutenant said. "And tie up Yellow Bird and that other one."

Three of the others were still alive, but dying. The burned Comanche was in agony from his wound and his burn, but the only sound that came from him was his panting. The burned skin was hanging from him in long narrow shreds. The stench made a couple of the men turn their heads away. Cpl. Schweizer came over and said, "Hurry up and die, damn you!" The warrior stared at him, and then turned his head looking for a weapon. There was nothing, not even a chunk of mesquite. He grabbed a handful of dust and flung it into the corporal's face. Schweizer kicked the Comanche in the stomach. He screamed a long "Ayyyyyy!" and died. Schweizer turned to the lieutenant and said, "Remember that private we found that day at the ford? It only took this Comanche five minutes to die."

The sergeant grabbed him by the arm. "Schweizer, some day! Listen, ride back and bring shovels."

Schweizer waited a moment, looking at Yellow Bird. In front of Yellow Bird was his lance, and from the top of it hung the scalps taken on this raid. He was now in a sitting position, his arms tied behind him. He caught the glances at the scalps. He said proudly, "Texas!"

"Schweizer!" said the sergeant, his voice filled with warning. The corporal turned and walked to his horse.

The lieutenant threw some water in the face of the other warrior, the one Christie had stunned with his rifle. He came to and held his head. The lieutenant searched among the pile of gear collected from the Comanches and found a small deerskin bag full of pemmican. He gave it to the Comanche. Then he said, "Sergeant, find him a pony. Make sure it's a poor one. I don't want to give away any good Government property."

The horse was brought up. The lieutenant untied the man's hands and motioned for the warrior to mount. He did so; it was evident he thought he was to be tortured in some unusual fashion. He pressed his lips together. "Goodbye," said the lieutenant, and slapped the horse. The horse shied, and then began to trot to the north. One of the troopers fired. The bullet kicked up a spurt of dirt near the horse's left rear leg; he broke into a fast gallop.

No one wanted any of the robes because of the bullet holes. Some of the troopers wanted bows and arrows for souvenirs; there was little else. One of the troopers found something and held it up. He said, "Hey, Lieutenant, you want this?" It was Yellow Bird's war bonnet. All the feathers were from the tail feathers of the young golden eagle. It looked magnificent cascading down in the firelight.

The lieutenant thought of Mrs. Anson. He said, "Yes, thanks. I'd like it." The trooper gave it to the lieutenant together with its buckskin bag. Yellow Bird looked at him. His face showed nothing, but his black eyes were searching everywhere—for a weapon, a knife, signs of another war party.

They found a human finger necklace, and a buckskin bag with twelve of the right hands of little babies of the Osage.

Before dawn the Indians were buried. The men had found twelve scalps altogether. The sergeant explained that the custom was to bury them. "Bury them then," the lieutenant said, "in a separate grave. And put a cross on it."

Yellow Bird was made to mount a horse. His ankles were tied together with rawhide under the horse's belly. The men had gone out in all directions hunting horses, but it had not taken them long to round them up, and with a trooper on each side of Yellow Bird, the patrol headed back for Fort Brill.

On the trip back Yellow Bird spoke only once. He said, "Welles catch me, me hang. Me catch him, he die."

TEN

The third cavalry was in the middle of the salute to the standard when Lt. Stowe's patrol entered Fort Brill.

From across the parade ground they heard the "Draw Saber!" and saw the blades flash. At "Present Saber!" Yellow Bird seemed to look with faint interest at the precision of the blades sweeping to the upright position, and when the major called "Trumpeter, sound 'To the Standard'!" Yellow Bird stared at the flag riding by the regiment. He obviously thought it was a religious symbol.

When the ceremony was over, Lt. Stowe brought the patrol up to the Administration Building. Lt. Wynn was leaning against the rail, smoking, and staring at Yellow Bird. The band began to play "Oh, Susanna!" Yellow Bird did not turn his head in the slightest. He was naked except for a breechclout, leggings and beaded moccasins. His head was bruised where Sgt. Christie had struck him with the rifle butt. The thong binding his ankles was removed and he was pulled off his horse and walked into the Administration Building.

After a moment, Major Welles entered. "Lieutenant

Stowe," he said, "will you come in and give me your report?" They walked into the major's office.

A few officers came in, laughing and smoking, and looked curiously at Yellow Bird. Pease walked in; he had been sent for by the major to act as interpreter. Yellow Bird looked at him. He did not like Pease, and his contemptuous face showed it. He asked, "Are we going to talk?" Pease nodded.

Yellow Bird held out his hands. "I cannot speak with these things on my wrists," he said. "You make me a squaw."

Pease said, "Only the major can order them taken off."

Yellow Bird asked, "When will they torture me?"

Pease said, "They will not torture you. You will have a trial. They have a paper which says you killed the people on the wagon train. They will read this paper in Texas and ask you questions and if the council thinks you killed those people in the wagon train they will hang you, and if they think some other chief did those things they will let you go."

Yellow Bird said, astonished, "Who speaks of a paper? I led in that raid, and if any other chief claims the honor of leading that party he will be lying to you. I led it myself."

"But you must not say that," said Pease. "Then they will surely hang you. You must be quiet and make them prove that you led in that raid." Yellow Bird's face was bewildered.

Major Welles entered. "Untie him," he said. The thongs were removed, and Yellow Bird began to rub his wrists. Major Welles had the dying statement of the private of the escort in his hands and he began to read it.

"Is that the paper?" asked Yellow Bird, interrupting.

"Yes," said Pease. "You must be still until Major Welles has finished reading it."

"I do not want to hear any more," said Yellow Bird. "I led in that raid."

"Wait a moment," said the major. "Does he understand that he is not to admit that if he wishes to go free?"

"I told him that."

"Why all this talk?" asked Yellow Bird. "I led that raid. I have repeatedly asked for arms and ammunition which have not been furnished. I have made many other requests which have not been granted. You do not listen to my talk. The white people are preparing to build a railroad through my country. This will not be permitted. Some years ago they took us by the hair and pulled us close to Fort Brill and it is farther now to raid into Texas.

"But all that is played out now. I want you to remember that. On account of these grievances, a short time ago, I took thirty of my warriors to Texas. I wanted to teach them how to fight. We found a wagon train and killed twelve of the men."

Far away across the parade ground the band began to play "Garry Owen."

The major listened a moment and said, "How many scalps did you take?"

"I took five at the wagon train," Yellow Bird said proudly, "and this time into Texas we stole only twenty horses. This was not a good raid for horses."

The major said, "I am sending you down into Texas to stand trial for the murders of: Philip Knapp, Robert O'Donnell, David Altman, Michael Gillen, Asa Clark."

Yellow Bird said, "I told you I did not want to listen to this."

". . . Gerard Cantwell, Robert Sullivan . . ."

"Why do you keep talking?"

"Mr. Pease, tell him he must listen to these names."

Yellow Bird subsided. When the major had read the list of the dead teamsters, he asked Yellow Bird, "Where are the prisoners?"

"In our lodges to the north." He added, defiantly, "How do you like the answer?"

"Take him to the guardhouse," said the major. "He will go tomorrow for trial in Texas. Lieutenant Stowe,

I want you to bring him down. Take one wagon for him, and another for supplies; take as many troopers as you want for an escort."

The lieutenant said, "Yes, sir."

Major Welles nodded. "Nice job, Lieutenant." He started to enter his office.

"Welles!" said Yellow Bird. The major stopped. "The young chiefs will all fight you. The old chiefs are old women. They cannot hold us back forever. There will be war to the knife!"

The major said slowly, "You shall have it, till every warrior cries enough."

The sergeant said, "All right, Yellow Bird. March!"

Yellow Bird turned and walked across the parade ground.

ELEVEN

The lieutenant took ten troopers with him. And since the Osage scouts had come back, apologized, and were looking for work, he decided to take six of them along also. It would take three days to get to Bitter Creek, where the trial would be held.

One small buckboard held Yellow Bird and his guard, Pvt. Wheaton. The other held food, blankets and tents. Lt. Stowe paired each Osage with a trooper. At first the troopers were sullen about not being permitted to ride next to their usual partners, but after an hour they got used to the situation and began talking or trying to learn sign language.

Pvt. Wheaton sat in the buckboard opposite Yellow Bird, whose hands were handcuffed before him. Since the morning was chilly a blanket had been draped across his shoulders. Wheaton held a loaded carbine across his knees. Leading the patrol rode the sergeant and the lieutenant. The buckboard with the supplies followed the one holding Yellow Bird, and to the front and rear rode the troopers and the Indian scouts.

They had come fifteen miles out of Fort Brill by noon. They stopped then and ate, and rode again. Yellow Bird refused to eat. After a while he said to George Washington: "Listen! I wish to send a message by you to my people. Tell my people that I am dead. I died the first day out from Fort Brill. My bones will be lying by the side of the road. I wish my people to gather them up and take them home. I wish my father to know this. He is Kicking Bird."

Then he covered his head with his blanket and began to sing: "Iha hyo ay iya o iha yaya . . ."

Some of the troopers turned and grinned. Sgt. Christie said, "Lieutenant, you better watch Yellow Bird. He's going to give you trouble."

The lieutenant swung around on his saddle and looked. "How do you know?"

"Because he's singin' his death song. Somethin' about 'Oh sun, you remain forever'."

The lieutenant looked carefully at Yellow Bird. He was sitting quietly and chanting under the blanket. "You put on the handcuffs yourself, didn't you?" asked the lieutenant.

"Yes."

"Well, better go back anyway and take a look." The sergeant started to drop to the rear. At this point Yellow Bird threw off his blanket. He had been trying to work the handcuffs off his wrists all morning. He saw he would not be able to do it: they were too tight. Shreds and strips of flesh hung down from his bleeding palms, and he realized that Wheaton, his guard, would notice the bloody floorboards any moment. He threw off his blanket and lunged at Wheaton, who saw him coming and half rose, but before he could do anything Yellow Bird had pulled Wheaton's .45 from his holster and shoved him. Wheaton was off balance and the struggle caused him to do a back somersault out of the wagon onto the dusty road. His faint yelp of surprise was drowned out by the rattle of the buckboard on the uneven road ruts.

Yellow Bird stood erect, and facing Lieutenant Stowe, had just aimed when Christie fired his Colt. The force of the .45 slammed him half way around so that he fired into the air. He tried once more but the sergeant's next shot blew open his neck. Yellow Bird let the .45 drop with a clatter to the wagon floor. He threw up both of his bleeding hands to his throat to hold back the blood; then he sank to his knees, choking. Most of the patrol had drawn their guns by now, the buckboard had halted, and his black eyes stared in hatred at the carbines that ringed him around. He opened his mouth to say something, but fell onto his back and died.

One of the scouts dismounted directly into the buckboard, and drew his knife. He grabbed Yellow Bird's braids and pulled his head around.

"Stop him!" said the lieutenant. Pvt. Wheaton was in the wagon, wiping the blood off his carbine. He pumped the lever and shoved the muzzle into the Osage's side. The scout let go the braids and Yellow Bird's head thumped onto the floor. Wheaton winced but kept the carbine steady. By this time the lieutenant was alongside. The Osage were talking angrily.

George Washington said, "They want scalp. Why no get scalp? Yellow Bird no want it." He grinned.

"You can't have it, and that's that."

George Washington stared at him. "Mebbe so, yes," he said.

The lieutenant said, "Pvt. Wheaton, shoot that scout if he makes a move toward Yellow Bird." He turned to George Washington. "And I'm going to shoot you next."

George Washington looked at him thoughtfully. Then he said, "You give us his blanket?"

"That you can have," said the lieutenant. "Wheaton, throw him the blanket."

While the patrol dug a grave for Yellow Bird the Osage divided the bloody blanket; each scout received an equal part which he thrust into his pouch for good medicine.

As soon as the patrol arrived back at Fort Brill the

lieutenant went directly up to the Administration Building. The major was in his office, and he listened in silence. When the lieutenant finished he shrugged, and said, "I don't blame him. I'd rather be shot myself. Just write up your report and when you're finished you can have a three-day pass. If you want it."

"I'll take it, sir."

"There's a small chance you might run into a war party," said the major, "but I don't think they'd come between the Fort and San Anselmo, especially if they're loaded down with horses. Still want to go?"

Lt. Stowe said yes. "Fine," said the major. "Have a good time. Tear up the town. You'll need the change. There's something big on the way I want you to do, and you'll need your relaxation. The moon raids have helped, but not enough, not enough at all. But don't worry about that now. Want to borrow some money?"

"No, sir. I have enough."

"All right. You can leave as soon as you put your report on my desk." The lieutenant went to his quarters and wrote his report. When he finished he stepped outside and almost walked into Sgt. Christie.

"I hear you got yourself a three-day pass, Lieutenant," he said. The lieutenant had, years ago, accepted the miracle of Army grapevine. He nodded. The sergeant went on. "If you'd like me to show you around, Lieutenant . . ."

The lieutenant said he thought it would be fine. "How about us ridin' over after retreat?" The lieutenant agreed. He walked across the parade ground and once more entered the major's office. He placed his report on the desk.

The afternoon had turned warm and Lt. Stowe decided to swim in the river instead of taking a shower. He went to his quarters and put on an old shirt, trousers, and a pair of moccasins he had picked up after the ambush of the war party.

He cut back of the stables. Christie was shaving, his suspenders hanging down to his knees. In the tangled mass of black hair on his chest several white hairs stood out. A large mirror hung from a nail driven into the stable wall and a few idle troopers stood up when they saw the lieutenant. He motioned for them to sit again.

"Whaddya think of these, Lieutenant?" Boo said, motioning to the hairs with his razor. "I just found 'em. They'll get me more respect from the young lieutenants, is all." He shaved a few strokes. "I'm gonna let my enlistment run out. I said it before. This time I mean it."

The sergeant resumed his shaving, and the lieutenant went on toward the river, down through the young willows and along the cottonwoods. There was a place where the river had dug itself a small cove and where a massive old cottonwood had sent one great limb straight out over the water for twenty feet before it curved gently upward.

Here the water was still and the leaves along the branch made a green lustre in the water. He scuffed through a bed of dry leaves, undressed and dove in. Five minutes later he was dressed and walking out. Where the edge of the grazing meadows met the young alders, he heard voices. They belonged to Beth, Crane in the Sky, and her daughter. The lieutenant stepped out of the thicket. The three of them were startled. They all turned and stared, alert and tense, like black-haired deer, and they sank back into relaxation.

"You came at us too quietly," Beth said.

"It's my moccasins."

She dropped her eyes to them. Then she looked at him. He stood, tall, his hair wet and curled in tight little spirals on the back of his neck, and his face tanned and thinned from the hard scouting of the past month. A few drops of water slid down his cheek.

"Sit down," she said, "while I tell a fairy story to Swift Otter." Swift Otter was waiting for the story, her legs crossed like tailors' legs, her elbows in her lap, and her chin resting on her open palms.

"And so Old Cannibal Owl," Beth said, "grabbed the little girl in his claws and flew, quiet as snow, to the Ghost Mountains." Beth opened and closed her fingers like claws, and pretended to grab Swift Otter, who squealed and buried her face in her mother's skirt. Her hair was braided and coiled atop her head, and this, coupled with her earrings, made her look strangely grave and mature.

After she had finished the story, Beth said, "Sam, will you have dinner with us tonight?"

"I'm going to San Anselmo," he said.

Her face stiffened. "I have a three-day pass," he added, "and I intend to stay there for three days."

She asked, "What can you do in San Anselmo that will take three days?"

"I intend to find out," said the lieutenant. He walked across the meadows. Near his quarters he saw Cross. He was in no mood to talk, but Cross turned and saw him.

He came toward the lieutenant. "Afternoon, Lieutenant," he said. "I hear you've been doin' some good work lately." The lieutenant kept on walking without slackening his speed. Cross kept pace. "Looks like you'll have more to do, too. I see them maneuvers all day, and I see the gear and rifles comin' in.

"Well," Cross said, "I'll have to slow up here; goodbye, Lieutenant, but I think you and I should have a nice private talk, real soon . . ."

The lieutenant grunted. He entered his quarters, and in fifteen minutes he and Christie were riding out the gate. "We're going to need this rest," said the lieutenant. "The major's got something lined up right afterwards."

"Another patrol?"

"I don't think so. He seemed too mysterious for just another patrol. Something big, I think."

"I can't think when I'm thirsty, Lieutenant. Besides, it ain't no use tryin' to figure his schemes out. He's too smart. So how about gettin' into San Anselmo a bit faster?''

They cantered the rest of the way.

TWELVE

San Anselmo was a dusty town with one windmill and two streets. The river bank was lined with willows and the rears of the town's four saloons were built on stilts to allow the flood water to pass below in springtime.

In San Anselmo almost everyone wore a gun. The corrals were well and strongly built, the houses of adobe, and enough carbines could be brought into play at any moment of the day or night to make any Comanche raid costly for the raiders. The result was that San Anselmo had always enjoyed immunity during the Comanche moons.

There were a few horses at the hitching posts. Some had the Rocking Horse brand, and some were unbranded; these belonged to two thirsty buffalo hunters who had just bought them from the Cheyenne.

Sgt. Christie said, "Saloons last, Lieutenant. The first thing is a hotel. When we pass out we wanna do it in our own home. Ain't nobody gonna watch us sleep it off behind a dirty saloon."

"A wise statement," said the lieutenant. The lieutenant had never slept it off in a saloon, but he was willing to admit it might happen. The hotel had a big double bed available. There was no wallpaper. There were seventy-four holes in the ceiling. The proprietor said they were shot there by two cowpunchers from the Rocking Horse ranch one dull Sunday morning. They were shooting at flies, he said.

The sergeant examined the sheets and mattress carefully, heedless of the proprietor's insulted looks. He said, "Don't look like no wild life here, Lieutenant."

They paid for the room, stabled their horses, and gave the proprietor five dollars more than he asked for. He wanted to know what it was for. "Why," said the sergeant kindly, "that's for the trouble we're gonna cause you when we come home tonight."

They walked down the street and into the Texas Star. "This has to be done right," said the sergeant, "from the beginning." He ordered a steak apiece, with bread, butter, potatoes and milk. "We are not gonna put any panther juice on an empty stomach," he said. "I want this toot to last considerable on my two months' pay and leave a pleasant feelin' in my mouth when I come to three days later. And, Lieutenant . . ."

"Yes, Sergeant?"

"If I can't, will you deliver the body to Fort Brill?"

The lieutenant said he would. They had three beers apiece waiting for the steak. A few cowpunchers had drifted in by this time and looked at them curiously. The Third U.S. had a poor record for amiability where citizens were concerned.

The soldiers ate their steaks. They had some bourbon. They decided to move on to the next saloon.

In the street they saw Cross riding. He saw them at the same time and rode over. "Lt. Stowe," he said, "can I talk to you?"

"Make it fast," said the lieutenant.

"I suggest the Lieutenant and me have a drink."

Lt. Stowe was in a good mood. He shrugged and they went in.

From the bar came Dimpdin's deep roar of "Gentlemen!" Christie grinned and walked over and began talking to him.

Cross was frank. "Lieutenant," he said, "I ain't a gentleman by Act of Congress, but I know a few things about human nature. And the first thing I learned is how easy it is for people to like you if you got money. The major don't like you too much, thinks you're not good enough for his daughter.

"It's money that does it. And I can get you plenty of it. And when you have plenty of it show me the man who won't think you'll make a fine son-in-law. He don't exist. Now, you just listen to me. I can get you plenty of money, and no one the wiser. I'll be honest with you—you don't get a lot of money unless you break a law. But there's one thing about me—I know how to keep my mouth shut. Nobody knows except me—and nobody sees me give you the money—you don't have to sign nothing. It's perfect. You come to the major with all that money in your hand—you're goin' to tell me he'll turn you down? You can say you won it gamblin'. Or that your uncle left it to you. It's good cash. It's clean cash—and no smell sticks to money. All money smells good—remember that. What do you say?"

"Go on."

"Comanches pay good for carbines," said Cross. "Damn good. Even in peacetime they paid plenty. And now—even more."

"I don't understand," said the lieutenant slowly. "Are you suggesting that I steal Army carbines and sell them to the Comanches?"

"Lord, no!" said Cross. "I wouldn't ask no officer to steal Army supplies! What I got to say is this: I got friends in Washington who'll ship me carbines. Comanches will pay twice or even three times as much for them now. But the trouble is there ain't no Comanches around close now. What I say is, sooner or later you'll be in a position to talk to some of 'em. I'll give you ten dollars for each carbine they take. Not enough? That's sort of a talking price. Maybe we can make it more later. And that's good money. No young officer on the frontier could make money like that.

"And if I got a shipment goin' through, why, you'll just look the other way if you run across it on patrol. I'll let you know in advance first where it's comin' from, so you don't even have to meet it. I'll pay you five dollars for each of the carbines you let through that way, and I want you to know I'm bein' honest about the whole thing, so I'll let you see the invoices for the carbines. Now! I ask you—could a man be fairer than that?"

"You're lucky you've still got a broken nose," said Lt. Stowe. "If you didn't I'd drive this glass in your face." He stood up.

Cross grinned, and said softly, "Calm down, Lieutenant. I always say 'Lieutenant.' I know my etiquette good. But all I gotta do is tell the major I seen you and his daughter comin' out of the sunflower patch—"

The lieutenant had sat down again beside him, and Cross, thinking he had decided to listen to reason, had relaxed his guard. But Lt. Stowe had sat down so he could meet Cross on an equal basis, and he hit Cross on the jaw as hard as he could. He went over backwards, and when he hit the floor he was unconscious.

The sergeant strolled over with Mr. Dimpdin, and looked down judiciously. "Very nice, Lieutenant," he said.

"Excellent," said Dimpdin in his richest bass. "May I buy a gentleman a drink?"

"You will be our guest, sir," said Lt. Stowe. "I suggest a place where Mr. Cross is not."

They left and went to the next place. "Three Monongohela!" said Lt. Stowe.

"A pleasure, sir," said Dimpdin. He drank his swiftly, then ran his tongue, long and thin and red, around the inside of the shot glass. He sighed. He said he was staying in San Anselmo for three days. He was preaching, he said. He also did something else to bring in money. He had a terrific specialty. "I am the scarer of naughty children," he said. "I charge fifty cents a child. The way I manage children is simple. First, I have to be alone with them, locked in a room. Then I look at them and talk to them. If they don't appear to come around, I tell them I have to put them up the chimney; and sometimes I have to put them up, a little. Yes, I make boys good. It's my business. I have two appointments now. Excuse me, gentlemen." He lifted his hat, bowed, and left.

"I like friend Dimpdin," said the lieutenant.

They heard someone playing a guitar in the early dusk. They were both just a little drunk by this time, nothing serious, and they left the bar and sat under a cottonwood and listened. All they could see of the singer was a huge pair of Mexican spurs banging gently against each other, keeping time. They belonged to a vaquero who was lying on his back on a bench back of the other saloon. He sang, *"Me abandonastes, mujer,"* and a few other songs in the soft and poignant tenor of Mexico.

He finished and lit a cigarette, and tapped the guitar gently with his brown fingers. Then he offered the soldiers some. They took them, and the sergeant said, *"Ay, que lindo, amigo! Haganos el favor de tomar algo con nosotros."*

The vaquero said he would be enchanted. He rose, and as they walked into the saloon, his enormous spurs jingled. They sat down and ordered. The lieutenant said he didn't know the sergeant could speak Spanish. "I once went into Mexico chasin' Apaches under MacKenzie," said the sergeant, "and in the retreat I was in the rear guard. There was a girl in Los Moras. . . . Three months later I came back. I said I had been captured and escaped. The captain I had then didn't believe me much, because I had gained twenty pounds, but he couldn't prove nothin'."

They drank some more. The vaquero said he was lonely, and here he was working for the Rocking Horse. The lieutenant was beginning to feel very good, and he invited the four cowpunchers at the bar to drink with them. They did. Then they all had another one. By now the lieutenant was beginning to feel a little dizzy, so he put his head in his arms.

The two buffalo hunters came in and boasted a bit. The lieutenant heard them faintly as if they were many rooms away, and then he heard one of them say, "But he don't look like much," and then he heard Boo's voice, in answer, saying: "It don't matter if the Indians have a day's start on him. He'll follow their trail to the jumping-off place and when he gets through with them the ground will be tore up, the bushes bit off, and blood, hair, livers and lights will be scattered all around."

The lieutenant vaguely realized Boo was talking about him. The other buffalo hunter said, "Yeah? He still don't look like much." The lieutenant was very sleepy and didn't care what the buffalo hunter said.

It was quiet for a moment and then he heard a sharp click! It was the sound two dice make rattling against one another. Then there was a thud. He looked up and saw Boo sitting down rubbing his knuckles. One of the buffalo hunters was dragging out the other by his heels. "I never liked the way them people killed buffalo anyways," said Boo to the vaquero, who did not understand English.

"*Si,*" gravely said the vaquero.

The spurs of the unconscious buffalo hunter kept catching in the rough pine planks of the floor and Boo said kindly, "Wait a minute." He got up, pulled off the boots and set them carefully on the man's stomach. The buffalo hunter continued to drag his friend out.

"If you get into any more trouble," said the lieutenant drowsily, "I shall have to restrict you to barracks."

"Yes, sir," said Boo.

Everyone had another drink. One of the cowpunchers looked Boo up and down very carefully, and then he sighed.

"You must think you're very tough," he said.

"Oh, my, no," said Boo.

"Oh, yes," said the cowpuncher. "I can tell. Are you from Texas?"

"No, sir," said Boo, "Mississippi."

"Ain't no one allowed to be tough in Texas 'ceptin' Texans," said the cowpuncher morosely, "and even then they're lookin' for trouble." He was a large man with a red pockmarked face. He removed his sombrero and gunbelt and set them neatly on the bar. "I don't like to do this, especially after we've done drunk your liquor, but I'm gonna have to teach you not to act tough in a Texas saloon."

"I would like to apologize," said Boo.

"Ain't no use," went on the cowpuncher. "What really worries me, though, is that I been your guest. Would you care for a drink as my guest first?"

"Honored," said Boo. He had one.

"And then," said the cowpuncher, "I don't like you drinkin' with that greaser from our ranch."

"Well, now," said Boo, "seein' that you stole Texas from these so-called greasers, I think you oughta start apologizin' yourself."

The lieutenant got involved in this one. Just before it started Boo grabbed the vaquero's knife and threw it so he couldn't use it. It stuck in the elaborate carved frame of the mirror over the bar. The bartender put on his coat, scooped up the silver dollars from the till, and began to move the chairs and tables and to stack them in a remote corner of the saloon.

The vaquero, although deprived of his favorite weapon, did well. He scratched and did some biting, and pulled hair somewhat. The lieutenant, in spite of the bourbon he had been drinking, got in a few good ones. This recompensed him for the black eye and the kick in the ribs he got. When the fight was well along, Boo seized the kerosene lamp, yelled, "A dark room and a bloody fight!" and threw it out into the street.

The best part was when two cowpunchers hit Boo at

the same time. He went backwards, crashed through a window that had not been washed since it was put in, and did a neat back somersault into the Red River. He came up, struck out for shore, walked around to the front of the saloon, and entered, refreshed.

The bartender came back with the sheriff and a new kerosene light. "Now look here, fellers," he said. "Why don't you be nice and go home? Please?"

"Fine!" said Boo. "What's the damage tonight?"

The bartender had a list all ready. He read off: "One mirror, three chairs, one kerosene light, one window, and thirty-nine shots of bourbon."

"Add it up," said the sergeant, "but deduct the window. I ain't gonna pay for the window. It ain't fair I get socked through a window I gotta pay for it."

The sheriff nodded. "That seems fair," he said. The bartender crossed out the window, and totalled the figures once more. "That comes to a hunnerd and thirty-two dollars this time, Sergeant."

Boo took a roll of bills from his pocket. He pulled off the required amount. Then he took out another ten and said, "Here's ten for the loan of your saloon." He turned to the lieutenant. "Lieutenant," he said, "let's go get a drink someplace."

The lieutenant said he was very sleepy and besides his eye hurt. The sergeant took him out into the street, walked him back to the river, and plunged his head in. After a few moments the lieutenant felt better. Then they made their way back to the street.

"Sergeant," said the lieutenant, "when we started out you had only two months' pay on you. Right?" The sergeant nodded.

"Well?"

"Well," he said, "them cowpunchers just been paid off. I threw the light out and then I would hit one hard in the dark and while he was resting I would get a contribution from him. Then I would get me another travelin' bank and do it again. I hadda get smacked hard a few times doin' it, but I collected over two hundred dollars after I threw the light out.''

"I'm very very sleepy," said the lieutenant.

"We have to go to this here place first," said the sergeant.

"Which here place?"

"This one," said the sergeant. They entered. When the madam saw Christie dripping wet and the lieutenant's black eye she grew angry, but the sergeant gave her fifty dollars immediately.

"In that case," she said. There was a real sofa and a real carpet. The lieutenant sat down on the sofa and hung his legs over one end and put his head on the cushions. Boo opened the lieutenant's collar.

"Evenin', Ma'am," he said. "Are you the lady they call the Great Western?" She nodded. She was over six feet tall and she weighed a hundred and eighty-five pounds. "I heard of you, Ma'am," he said. He leaned toward her and took a deep breath. "Ummmmm," he said happily. "Perfume."

"Like it?" she asked. "I keep a sachet of it here." She pulled it out from the inside of her decolletage a bit and leaned over. Boo said, "Ooh."

There were big blue circles under her eyes, but her chest development was admirable. "Mrs. Old Cannibal Owl," murmured the lieutenant.

"What's the matter with the lieutenant?" she asked.

"He don't hold liquor too good," said the sergeant, embarrassed.

"Also," she said critically, "he looks somewhat stomped on."

"There's that, too," agreed the sergeant.

The lieutenant heard all this vaguely, but he was too sleepy to stir. Suddenly he felt Boo shaking him. "Lieutenant," he said, "look at this!"

The lieutenant opened his eyes. "Watch now," said Boo. He gave the Great Western a five dollar bill. She folded it slowly till it was a small square. Then, very slowly, she pulled up her dress till a white and handsome thigh was thoroughly exposed. She inserted the folded bill in her stocking top and let the skirt fall again.

"That's the greatest thing I ever saw," said Boo, aghast. He gave her another five. She repeated the whole thing again. "Wonderful," said Boo. He stuck his hand in his pocket again.

The lieutenant went to sleep.

"Listen, Lieutenant," Boo was saying, "loan me five, will you?"

"Take it," said the lieutenant. He fell asleep again.

He woke to hear her say, "You ought to be ashamed of yourself for that indecent suggestion, but go upstairs and take off them wet clothes."

"Can't leave my lieutenant," Boo said stubbornly. "Army regulations."

"Dismissed," said the lieutenant.

"I have a girl from St. Louis for your friend," said the Great Western. "Her father is a big brewer and she's only nineteen."

"Look," said the sergeant, "maybe them ignorant cowpunchers go for that, but the only reason any girl works out here in these places is because she's ninety years old and tired of life on the farm."

The madam laughed. They got the lieutenant upstairs. She carried his legs easily, and he felt a huge crackling bulge on her thigh, under her stocking top. He fell asleep immediately. He woke up hours later. It was morning. It was quiet and chilly, but warm under the blankets. A pretty girl was looking down at him. She was wearing only a wrapper and a pair of scuffed red slippers. She was not nineteen, but she was not ninety either. "Later," said the lieutenant. He fell asleep again. When he woke up again it was mid-morning. His clothes were neatly hung in the closet and she was beside him.

"What's your name?" he asked.

"Elsie."

"Did I?" he asked.

"No," she said.

"Good morning," he said, and fell asleep once more. He woke up an hour later. He put out a hand. Elsie was still there, asleep. She felt round and warm, and she smelled clean. She woke up under his touch. She turned out to be very accomplished.

THIRTEEN

Three days later they rode out of San Anselmo. Sometime in those three days the sergeant had acquired a big roll of Mexican pesos which everyone had refused to accept, and from time to time he pulled it out and looked at it, puzzled. The lieutenant, in the same three days, had added a small cut over his left eye, and someone had hit him again on his black eye. His knuckles, he had discovered, were scraped raw. This gave him the comfortable feeling that he had acquitted himself well. He knew he hadn't scraped them when he hit Cross.

The sergeant had a small area on the top of his skull shaved and daubed with iodine. But their uniforms were clean and freshly pressed, and a small rip in the sergeant's left sleeve, where someone had swung a Bowie knife at him, had been neatly stitched. This repair work was the gift of the Great Western, who had also staked them to one more night at her place, no charge, when it was discovered they had no money left. "And furthermore," said the sergeant, "she gimme a dollar to tip the stable boy and a big kiss for myself. Was Elsie nice?"

"Elsie was nice," said the lieutenant. "I wouldn't exactly say she broke into tears when I left, but Elsie was nice."

"That's nice," said the sergeant.

They rode for a while, contented. Then the lieutenant said, "What happened to that vaquero?"

"What vaquero?"

"You know what vaquero." The sergeant wore a baffled expression. The lieutenant continued: "Don't you remember? He's the one who scratched up the face of that Rocking Horse cowpuncher." Still the sergeant shook his head. Then his glance fell on the big wad of pesos that bulged out his pocket. "Well, now," he said, blushing. "I guess when I threw out that lamp I got indiscriminate."

They were quiet for about a mile. Then the sergeant asked, "Your conscience bother you any?"

The lieutenant thought. Finally he said, no, it didn't. "Sometimes," said the sergeant, "I'm worried. Mine leaves me alone."

"I feel fine," said the lieutenant.

"You know, this business we're in," said the sergeant, "all you get is a blue hole where the forty-five went in, a cross on the prairie, and if you're lucky, someone in the patrol who knows the Twenty-third Psalm. If I had any sense I'd get out of it."

As they dismounted at the stables, Lt. Wynn ran up. "There's always excitement when you're around, it seems like," he said, breathless. "We're going on an escort. Me too. The major asked to see you as soon as you came in. Where did you get the lovely eye?"

"It was either the Texas Star or the Longhorn," said the lieutenant, as he started to walk up to the Administration Building. "Or was it somewhere between? You should've been along."

The major was waiting. He had been drinking, but was in fine control of his diction. He leaned back in his chair and looked at the battle damage. "What did it cost?" he asked critically.

"A hunnerd and thirty-two bucks," said the sergeant, pleased.

"Hmmm," said the major; he seemed jealous.

"Yours was less, sir," said the sergeant.

"Mind your manners, Sergeant," said the major.

"Sorry, sir."

"At ease. Did the sheriff write to Washington again?"

"No, sir. He just looked sad." The major grinned.

"Sir," said Lt. Stowe.

"Well, Lieutenant?"

"Cross came up to me in San Anselmo and asked me to look the other way when a shipment of his carbines for the Comanches would be coming in. He also offered me ten dollars apiece for each carbine I could sell."

"What did you say to that?"

"I hit him."

The major sighed. "Anyone hear him make the offer?"

"No one except me, sir."

"I would like to string the son of a bitch up as much as you would, but you forget two things. You don't have a witness, and you ruined a fine chance to play along with him and nail him with the goods. So forget about it."

"But aren't—"

"Lieutenant, if I say anything to him about it he'll say you're lying to get him in trouble because he tried to beat you up. There's nothing left for me to do except keep some sort of a watch on him, and we don't have any trained detectives on the post. He'll be twice as careful now, and it's going to be hard to pin evidence on him. And there's one more thing for you to remember—he has powerful friends in Washington. But I'll try." Then he reached into a drawer, pulled out a map, and said, "Take a look at this." They stood about the map and looked. The major's pencil wavered a bit and then touched a river. "This," he said, "is Buffalo Bone Ford. Two days to the north." Then his pencil moved westward and stopped. "And this," he added, "is Fort Martin. Our problem is to meet a certain McDonald who comes highly recommended with letters from Washington. You will meet

him, Lt. Stowe, at Buffalo Bone Ford. Mr. McDonald
and twelve men will have a few hundred horses with them.
McDonald's aim in life is to deliver them to California,
where they are fetching very fancy prices. If he does it,
and if he finds forage for them along the way, he will
wind up in Los Angeles a very rich man. And if he
doesn't—have a drink. Fine bourbon.''

"Thanks, sir,'' said Lt. Stowe.

Sgt. Christie looked sceptical. The major laughed. The
wind came in through the window and the map trembled;
he placed a hand over the Red River and the map grew
still, like a calmed horse.

"McDonald thinks the purpose of the trip is to deliver
horses. Let him think so. When I heard of this escort I
decided I had to use it as a decoy. As I was afraid might
be the case, the Comanches aren't coming out in force
on their moonlight raids. Thirty warriors here, fifty
there—at that rate it'll take us too long to wear them
down.

"When they see the terrific bait I've placed on the hook
for them with McDonald's help, they won't be able to
resist snapping at it. And once they do, you won't be able
to shake them off—even when they start losing men.
They'll be like sharks that smell blood.

"They won't dare make a rush all at once on all you
well-armed men. And even if they do—well, you'll just
have to handle it.

"They'll probably content themselves with sniping, ambush, things like that. Maybe try to stampede the horses.
But you'll wear 'em down quick. I know I'm risking some
civilian lives, with all those herders McDonald has along,
but they'd be in danger anyway, and I never expected to
make colonel. And with our superiority in fire power we'll
really be in a position to do some big damage.

"Well,'' he said, suddenly gentle, "double your
insurance, keep your Colts oiled, and here's a letter for
Burton.''

He noticed Lt. Stowe's puzzled look. "Fort Martin's commander," he said. "We were up in the Crow Country together." He stood up and shook hands with the three of them.

Their road this time led to the north. First by the Anson Ranch where three-foot high weeds grew among the blackened beams, then up through country where not even the boldest rancher dared live.

They went up a steep hill, and suddenly, as if a curtain had risen, they came out upon a broad prairie, reaching, in swells like an ocean after a great storm, to the horizon before them. A thick screen of woods edged it on the distance to the left, and an open grove of low oaks broke upon it in an irregular line to the right, with spurs and scattered single oaks. They crossed capes and islands of the grove, sometimes with Spanish moss hanging from the lowest branches of the oaks that brushed against their faces.

The waves of the prairie went on. Four of the waves covered a mile, and as soon as they climbed to the top of one, the contour of the next appeared dark against the sky.

In the afternoon they found very little water, not much grass, and much broken ground. Toward dusk they passed by an abandoned sod house that some pioneer had cut out of the prairie years ago. Nailed to a piece of decaying plank was a sign:

"Toughed it out here two years: results: stock on hand, five towheads and seven yaller dogs. 250 feet down to water. 50 miles to wood and grass. Hell all around. Goin' back."

On one of the western ridges they saw smoke rising. "They're watching," said the lieutenant. "Drop back and don't let anyone straggle." Every once in a while the point reported that he saw distant riders who would not respond to his "I-want-to-talk" signals. Double guard was to be posted at night; big campfires were to be made, "In case," said the sergeant, dryly, "we got us some ninety-year-old blind Comanches out there." The men were tense after they saw the signal smoke.

At night, after they were asleep, and after Sgt. Christie had double-checked the sentries to be sure that they were paying attention to their business, the lieutenant raised up on one elbow and looked at the men, and then at the horses. There were the usual snores. For some reason the best soldiers snored the loudest, and this was a mystery that had haunted the lieutenant since he had joined the army as a boy of sixteen.

For a moment more the lieutenant lay awake looking at the sentries and the horses. One of the horses was eating grama grass; he stopped eating a moment, shook his mane, snorted softly, and began to eat again. Somehow the sound and the gesture, reminiscent of the old plow horses in the stable where he used to sleep on Sunday afternoons in summer when he was a boy, made the lieutenant feel immensely content and relaxed. He pulled his blanket high over his head and fell asleep.

About midnight Sgt. Christie woke up. There was a rustle from the back of one of the supply wagons, the one that held sugar. Since sugar was something that the troopers were always stealing on the march, he watched. It could also be a Comanche that had gotten past the double pickets. He quietly pulled his Colt from under his saddle, cocked it, and waited.

The canvas lifted up, a pair of legs slid over the tailgate, and the figure dropped to the ground on moccasined feet. They went by the sergeant. When they were close enough he hooked an ankle with his left instep and pushed the intruder's knee with his right foot. The figure went down and the sergeant said, "Don't move!" If it was a Comanche he would understand the cocked Colt.

"Boo!" said the figure.

"My God!" said the sergeant. It was Beth. "Oh, let me up now," she said. "I have to stretch." She got up and stretched, while the sergeant woke up Lt. Stowe. They stared at her. "I came," she said, "because I wanted to see Kitty."

"Kitty?" asked the lieutenant, bewildered.

"Kitty Burton. Her father is the commander at Fort Martin. I haven't seen her for two years."

She had hid in the back of the wagon at Fort Brill, she said. Her father didn't know, and he was leaving the next morning on a patrol for two or three days before her rising time, so he wouldn't know till he got back, and no one would come by the house for a day or so, and if they did, she had left a note explaining everything, so there was nothing to worry about.

"Nothing, eh?" said the lieutenant.

"Dad'll curse a bit, and he'll hope I'm all right. That's all."

"I can't spare anyone to take you back," said Lt. Stowe. "Any escort of five or six would be pretty sure to get wiped out." She was smiling. "Well, I hope you'll get to see Kitty."

The sergeant fed her, and she fell asleep by the fire while her bed was made ready in one of the wagons. Her single braid, like a Comanche girl's, came over her shoulder, like a thick black rope, and she slept as evenly as a candle burning.

At four the next afternoon the point galloped back and reported he had seen the herd at the rendezvous, which was at the foot of a three hundred-foot-high granite cliff. There was plenty of good grass at the base of the cliff and along the river on either side for a mile or so. The herd was grazing among the old buffalo bones that had given the ford its name.

When the escort was still a mile away McDonald came riding out to meet them. He was a small sour-faced man with smooth grey hair. He stuck out a small damp palm and shook hands. "Name's McDonald," he said, impatiently. "Been waitin'."

Lt. Stowe introduced himself and Lt. Wynn.

McDonald mumbled something in response, which neither officer could catch. Then he added, "You're in time for supper. Enough for all. Hope you'll join us."

McDonald's hunters had brought in some buffalo, and since he was traveling in style, the men sat down to a meal of buffalo ribs, mashed potatoes, hot corn bread, real butter, and apple pie and coffee. "Eat good," McDonald said gloomily. "It cost enough." They did.

Then he observed, "My men saw Indian sign about noon." Lt. Stowe put down his coffee cup. "Smoke signals, most like," went on McDonald. "To the north. Good coffee?"

"Fine," said Lt. Stowe. "Seen anything else?"

"No, just smoke."

"What makes you think it was Indian sign?"

"Men say it came in regular puffs."

The lieutenant said, "I'd like you to set your men in a double picket around the herd. Mine will make a line guard half a mile further out, with a few along the river in case someone might try to swim across. We'll leave half an hour after sunrise, so you better have somone pass the word to the cook."

McDonald said, "Look, Lieutenant, we better straighten this out right away. Does all this mean you're goin' to tell me when to get up, where to go, when to eat, how fast to travel, and when to stop?"

"That's about it," said the lieutenant.

"This is not a government operation," said McDonald. "This is a private affair, and I am a taxpayer askin' for protection and you are my servant and you are obliged to supply it. I don't see how it follows that you think you have to run everything."

Lt. Wynn flushed, said, "Look here . . ."

"Shhh," said Lt. Stowe. Wynn subsided. Lt. Stowe said, calmly, "There is going to be only one of us leading—me, or I'm taking back the escort."

"Look here, Lieutenant, I have a letter . . ."

"Oh, God, that letter!" The lieutenant rose. "Sergeant!"

Sgt. Christie rose from the bench where he was eating, his mouth stuffed. "Lieutenant?"

"Pack up, we're going back."

"Now?"

"Now!"

The sergeant swallowed, turned, and yelled, "All right, drop those cups, pack up and stand to horse! Snap to it!"

McDonald surrendered. "All right," he said wearily. "Tell 'em not to move."

"Is it understood I'm in command?"

"Yes, sure," said McDonald bitterly.

"I suggest then, we leave at sunrise."

"Mmmm," said McDonald. He turned and left.

As Wynn and Stowe folded their blankets and lay down, Lt. Wynn said, "You'll probably hear about this, Sam."

"Maybe. I doubt it."

"Maybe so, yes! He'll write to his friend the general, who will write to another general, enclosing copies, who will write to the general commanding the Army of the West, who will write to Edwards who will write to Welles, who will call you into his office . . ."

"Do you want to know why none of this is important?" asked the lieutenant. "If we get the herd there safely, and do what Welles sent us to do, who cares if he complains? And if we never get there, who cares what McDonald says? Good night."

"Good night, Sam."

FOURTEEN

All next day they saw no Indian sign. No smoke, no old campfires, nor did the scouts report anything moving except antelope and a few scattered buffalo.

The country was broken; very gradually it began to tilt upwards. There were many little streams which had cut themselves small ravines below the level of the surrounding prairie, and these had such steep sides that several times a day they had to be sloped off so that the wagons could cross them.

Most of these ravines were invisible till the herd was almost upon them. The point scouted these warily, but with confidence: it was well known that any ambush would let the lead scouts through and then jump the main body of the party. So there was some competition to ride point.

Late that afternoon they saw signal fires ahead. Lt. Stowe shaded his eyes against the afternoon sun and smiled.

"For a while there I was afraid we'd lost them. They seem, though, to have a pretty good idea where we're going, camping just ahead of us this way. You might even wonder if maybe somebody didn't give them our destination, say my friend Cross. No doubt he picked up wind about this escort, but not about its real mission.''

''Well,'' said the segeant, ''if Cross did tip them, he did us a favor and doesn't know it. Anyway, one thing's sure, his nose ain't gonna heal straight. I know because I hit it sort of sideways.''

Two days later they found poor grass and very little water. Towards evening they found a ravine deep and wide enough to hold all the horses. There was some grass in the bottom, but when the sergeant saw it he whistled. ''We call that 'Two Day Grass',''️ he said. ''A bellyful of that stuff keeps a tired horse travelin' two days more. But there ain't hardly a handful.'' There was a good growth of small cottonwood trees along the bottom of the ravine, however, and the horses were content, nibbling at the young shoots and the inner bark. When the herd had been driven in and the wagons turned sideways across the ravine mouth so that the ravine opening was effectively blocked, Lt. Stowe walked onto a large flat rock and sat down. The afternoon was hot and below the prairie level, out of the wind, it seemed midsummer. On the edge of the rock three tiny green lizards were panting in the heat; they stared at the lieutenant, quivering and ready to streak for cover if he moved in their direction.

''You think they'll make a jump tonight?'' asked the lieutenant.

Christie nodded. ''The huntin's been bad,'' he said. ''No buffalo, no antelope. They're followin' and they're hungry, and they're gettin' restless, I bet, and they want to end this. And all the horses we got must be drivin' 'em crazy. If I was a Comanche I'd make a try for 'em just about now, eat a couple of ponies—''

Lt. Stowe made a face.

''Horse ain't so bad, Lieutenant, I've et it. So I figure maybe they'll jump us tonight and feast themselves, and then go off home, wavin' our scalps. That's what's passin' through their minds right now, I bet, since their ponies must be growin' weaker day by day on the poor grass we been seein'."

"All right," said the lieutenant. He watched Lt. Wynn make his way up to the rock. "I want everyone to eat now and go to sleep. As soon as it gets dark I want everyone on watch, and I mean everyone, along the edge of the ravine on both sides. We'll keep watch that way all night long. Then if they don't jump us we'll shove off at sunrise and have a good sleep tomorrow night. Pass the word."

The sergeant nodded.

"Sergeant," asked Lt. Wynn, "did I hear you say you've eaten horse?"

"Yessir."

"Ugh," said Lt. Wynn.

"It ain't so bad, sir. It all depends on what kind you're eatin'. I've et horse bein' chased by Sherman in Georgia and it was awful. I've et it on patrol in Arizona, and it was better. It all depends. For instance, take cavalry horse, played-out and sore-backed. Well, that's leathery, stringy, and I don't mind sayin' it'd make even me puke. Then we try cavalry horse, younger and not too skinny— and that tastes like bad beef. You gotta eat that quick and holdin' your nose. And then it ain't too bad. But what I like is Indian pony, growed-up. That tastes like elk. And Indian pony, colt—that's the best, Lieutenant. It tastes like antelope."

"That's enough, Sergeant."

"Yes, sir. Mule is awful."

"That's really enough, Sergeant."

"Yes, sir." He rose and said, "I'll take a look at the men, Lieutenant."

"Go ahead," replied Lt. Stowe. Christie walked down the slope.

"You asked him, Wynn," said Lt. Stowe, mildly.

"I know, and I'm sorry."

They watched the men trying to sleep. Beth climbed the slope and joined them.

"What'll you do," asked Lt. Wynn, "when your father gets posted to Washington? You'll have to learn to ride sidesaddle like a lady."

She sat on the rock and began combing her hair. "I've never ridden sidesaddle in my life."

"That's how they tell who's a lady and who isn't," said Lt. Wynn.

"I won't be a lady," she said. "I hate Eastern saddles anyway. You slide all around them like buckshot in a bottle. Lieutenant Stowe," she added, "your views on Eastern saddles, please."

"I don't have any."

"That's a shame, Lieutenant," she said. "I wanted an expert's view on what I should look like riding sidesaddle in Washington. And you can't tell me."

"I can tell you," said Lt. Wynn. "You would look—" He began to tell her how wonderful she would look. Lt. Stowe said he had to look at the men, and he left. He thought that he had never seen her in a dress, but that if she were to wear a green gown . . .

Down below the sergeant was awakening the men. He was saying, very softly, "Come, boys, come. Get up and hear the little birds singing their praises to God. ALMIGHTY DAMN YOUR SOULS! GET UP!"

They got up. After a supper of beans, salt pork, and coffee, they were assigned their posts along the edge. The night went on without event, but everyone's nerves would have been better if something had happened.

In the morning they left the ravine and climbed the easy slope and headed west. Here an old fire had burned off the prairie for miles and the horses' hooves made soft little plopping sounds in the inch-thick blash ash. A few pools of rainwater were found, black with soot, and the horses who got there first had to be forced away to let the others drink. Some of the men drank also, but the water was so full of alkali that after a few hours of travel their lips had cracked open and blood began to trickle down their chins. Then the fire had reached a broad rock-strewn valley and had burned itself out; on the other side the dried prairie began again.

They followed that for a while. Then they came around the base of a low ridge and found a stream flowing along the bottom of the ridge and moving out into the flat land. The water was good, although there was little grass, just enough for a few hours' grazing.

Suddenly a warrior appeared on the ridge. He rode in zig-zags, and Lt. Stowe, who was riding behind the point with Lt. Wynn, said, "You know what that means, Wynn?"

Wynn shook his head. "He walks to talk," said Lt. Stowe. He rose in his stirrups, turned around, and waved for Sergeant Christie to ride up. Sergeant Christie caught the signal and spurred alongside. "I'm going out and powwow," said the lieutenant. "You fall behind me a bit and cover me, as you interpret."

Lt. Wynn said he wanted to go too. Lt. Stowe said, patiently, "Suppose it's a trick and they open fire and kill the both of us? Who takes the herd on to Fort Martin? McDonald? You'd be bad enough, but at least you know enough to hold everything together. I need Christie because he talks Comanche. All right, Sergeant, pick up Schweizer and have him stay fifty feet behind us."

Now they could see the Comanche clearly as his pony neared them. He wore a full-length war bonnet of eagles' feathers descending to his pony's tail, almost sweeping the ground. He wore large brass hoops in his ears. He was naked to the waist, and on his broad chest hung a necklace of grizzly bear claws that gently swung as he rode. He carried a lance that had several black pennants on it, and when he got within fifty feet they could see that the pennants were scalps.

He wore leggings, a breechclout, and moccasins with a pattern formed of blue and green beads. His scalp lock was braided with white otter fur and tied with bright red flannel. His pony's bridle was ornamented with bits of silver and in its tail and mane he had braided more red flannel.

Another pony rode up to the crest of the ridge where the Comanche had ridden from. Its rider wore the buffalo-headdress made out of buffalo horns. As he watched them and knew he was being watched he placed a palm on his forehead and turned it back and forth rapidly.

"War sign," said Christie. "Easy, Lieutenant."

The Comanche was almost up to them by now. He saw them looking behind him; he turned and saw the Comanche on the ridge. He lifted a hand and pressed it down almost as if he were forcing down the head of an unruly puppy. The Indian on the ridge grew motionless. Then the warrior turned and looked at Lt. Stowe. He had reached a small stream with a willow thicket at his side. He dismounted and waited for them to come up.

As they waded across, Lt. Stowe asked, "Recognize him?"

"No, sir," said the sergeant. "He wasn't at the powwow. He looks like one of the younger chiefs who wouldn't come. And the one up on the ridge looks young too. They're the ones who wouldn't listen to Tall Bear. Best be careful, Lieutenant. Yellow Bird said it would be war to the knife, and when they say that they ain't foolin'."

"I know. But we have a job to do, and maybe this will be our chance to get it over with. I want to provoke a fight, and this seems to be a good place for it. And from our point of view, for a change."

Lt. Stowe waded across the stream with Sgt. Christie. The Comanche removed his knife and placed it on the ground. Lt. Stowe pulled out his Colt and placed it on the ground, and did the same with his knife. The Comanche held his empty right hand up and out.

"I want your horses," he said in Comanche. "Give me your horses and I will let you go."

"I like my horses," said the lieutenant. "They are good horses. I will keep them."

"I know you," said the Comanche. "You are Stowe. You took away eighty horses from Hard Rope two moons ago. You are a good fighter. I am Spotted Crow."

"You are a dirty Indian," said Sgt. Christie suddenly in English. "You eat dog. Your sister sleeps with the soldiers for money."

"Sergeant!"

"It's all right, Lieutenant," replied the sergeant. "I want to see if he talks English. He don't. Look at him." Spotted Crow stood, calm and puzzled. The sergeant went on. "Lieutenant, like you said, we're in a good defensive position right now." The lieutenant nodded, and looked where the willow-fringed river came along the base of the ridge, and then edged out into the plain, where it made an ox-bow loop. In the area formed by the bend of the river grazed the herd. The herd filled the loop, penned in by the willows, and the only way out was barred by a small sandy hill, which ran between the loops of the river. "We could dig in mighty fast in that sand, Lieutenant. It would be pretty hard to stampede the horses across the river or up the hill, especially now that they're drinkin' that good water and feedin' on that good grass. It takes a lot to make a Comanche charge in the open in full daylight, even these young bucks, but maybe we can make 'em."

"How?"

"Oh tell 'em they're women. Try that first."

The lieutenant turned to the Comanche. "You followed us all the way. We saw your smokes. The hunting was bad. You look hungry."

The Comanche said nothing. "You do not look cunning to me," went on the lieutenant. "Cunning people do not starve." He ran his finger across the Comanche's ribs. The Comanche grew angry, both at the gesture and the statement.

"We are not fools," he said. "Fools have to watch your fort all the time to know when you leave. We know when you leave. We have a very good friend in your camp! We do not have to lie in the cold and see when you leave the fort. We have a friend who tells us these things."

"I do not believe you," said the lieutenant, trying to provoke the Comanche into anger. "What is his name?" He knew very well what the name was.

"You take me for a fool," said the Comanche, and would not speak further. But the lieutenant could see that he was getting angrier. Spotted Crow looked over their shoulders at the horses.

"That's some war bonnet he's got," said the sergeant. "Biggest one I ever saw."

"They're sacred, aren't they?"

"Yep. Somethin' like our flag and a statue of the Virgin Mary and the Medal of Honor, all at once."

"Good. You take over and tell Spotted Crow that he is a coward, that if he wanted the horses he should try and take them instead of begging for them like a coyote, that he hides when fighting is to be done. Pile it on."

Lt. Stowe could see by the reaction of Spotted Crow that the translation was accurate.

"Tell him anything unpleasant you can think up," Stowe added.

Sergeant Christie grinned happily and spoke some more. Spotted Crow listened a bit, then spoke angrily and too rapidly for the lieutenant. Christie listened and said, "He challenges you. Right now. You and him. Winner to take the other's horse and weapons. This never happened before, Lieutenant. If he gets to take your horse and carbine I'm gonna have a hell of a time explainin' to the major how come I let government property get away from me, not to mention why the hell I let you do it in the first place."

"All right, Sergeant. We came here to provoke a fight, and I'm going to do it. I don't want it tomorrow. We have too nice a defensive spot right here to waste. I want the fight right now and right here.

"Tell Lieutenant Wynn he takes command if I lose. Tell him I said to listen to you, and don't let McDonald run all over him. Tell Schweizer to ride back and have the men dig pits along the top of the hill right away."

"Listen, Lieutenant, this is against Army regulations; there ain't no such thing as single combat in the Army—"

"Sergeant, if he wins let him get back with his people without shooting him in the back. But when they attack do me a favor and get him. Promise me that."

"Sure, Lieutenant, but I—"

"That's all, Sergeant. Goodbye." The sergeant pulled his horse back a few feet and remained, stubborn as a small boy. "Get going, Sergeant." The sergeant looked at him, his face getting red, then he wheeled his horse and spurred it across the shallow river.

Spotted Crow took off his war bonnet and hung it carefully over his saddle horn. Then he took off his necklace of bears' claws and hung it on the horn. He took off his hoop earrings. The lieutenant took off his coat and his cartridge belt and hung them both on his saddle horn.

The Comanche pulled out a long string of rawhide from a small pouch that hung near his saddle horn. He picked up his knife and placed it in his knife scabbard and motioned for the lieutenant to do the same. He draped the rawhide across their left wrists, and bound their two left arms together with several turns, beginning at the elbows and ending at the wrists. When he finished he placed his right hand on the pommel of his knife and stared at the lieutenant for several seconds. The lieutenant could see a scar that began at the corner of his mouth, ran halfway across his face, and then slashed downward and cut back under his chin. He had obviously been in a knife fight before. Spotted Crow nodded and drew his knife, hooked his foot behind the lieutenant's left ankle, and pulled it toward him. The lieutenant went off balance and fell, dragging Spotted Crow on top of him with his bound left arm. He parried Spotted Crow's thrust as he fell, and forced Spotted Crow's wrist backwards till it was against his throat. He pressed even harder till the pressure of his forearm began to cut off the Comanche's breath.

Spotted Crow twisted his head to the right and swung his elbow around so that it hit the lieutenant in the mouth. A thin trickle of blood slid out. Then Spotted Crow forced the lieutenant's arm back and they slowly rose, wrists locked, to a sitting position. Spotted Crow slowly yielded his arm, maneuvering the lieutenant's right arm till it was within the grasp of Spotted Crow's bound left hand. Then his left hand grasped the lieutenant's right wrist, and with a sudden twist Spotted Crow's knife hand came free.

His knife flashed up and down. The lieutenant rolled sidewards. The blade sliced through his shirt and was buried to the hilt in the hard-packed earth. In the two seconds it took Spotted Crow to free his knife, Lt. Stowe struck. His blade grated on a rib. He struck again. This time the blade slid in smoothly, up to the hilt. It was in the heart; the lieutenant left it there and grabbed Spotted Crow's left wrist. The Comanche, realizing he did not have enough strength to pull out his knife, reached upwards with his bare hand and tried to claw out the lieutenant's eyes. He missed, and under his nails four parallel scratches sprang up on the lieutenant's right cheek. Then the Indian died.

The lieutenant lay there, panting. Up on the ridge he noticed, for the first time, many mounted warriors. One of them, in a buffalo horn headdress, shook his lance in grief and rage. The lieutenant cut the thong and stood up, wiping the blood from his face, shaking a bit. He buckled on his gunbelt, gasping. Then he wiped his knife by plunging it twice into the ground. He put it back in its scabbard. He took the necklace of bears' claws and shoved it in his pocket. He mounted his horse, reached over, took Spotted Crow's war bonnet from the saddle horn, and held it high in the air, shaking it at the warriors on the ridge. Several of them shook their lances at him. He reached down, pulled Spotted Crow's lance out of the ground, shook it at the ridge once, and then drove it into the ground, first ripping off two of the scalps that hung from it. He shook the scalps at the warriors, then, grabbing Spotted Crow's war pony by the reins, started back. The pony was shy of the Army horse and wouldn't come, but the heavier Army horse leaned into it and the pony was dragged, stubbornly at first, but later yielding. As he crossed the river he let the bonnet down till the end of it floated in the water, and as he reached the far bank he let it hang and drag on the ground. One warrior burst from the quickly increasing group on the ridge but a sharp command brought him back. Several of the chiefs were in council. A little below them the younger warriors watched, furious.

Suddenly the whole ridge was alive with horses. At each end of the ridge more mounted warriors emerged. There were warriors on brown and white ponies, black ponies, sorrels, greys, and others who were striped with black paint till they looked like zebras. Black ponies were never painted, but the rest were. They came at a fast trot till those from each end of the ridge had met with those coming down the ridge.

The lieutenant dismounted. "Get under the wagon and stay there," he told Beth. Lt. Wynn had made a good disposition of his men; several had been placed among the thick willows so that they could pick off anyone attempting to get to the horses and stampede them, the rest of the men well hidden in rifle pits strung along the top of the hill. Their ammunition was carefully laid out beside them. The medical orderlies were ready by the wagons, and all the men had their canteens freshly filled with water.

The Comanches splashed across the shallows. One of the chiefs leaned down and pulled out Spotted Crow's lance as he rode by. They forced their way through the willows, and emerged on the flat land. For a moment they stopped, motionless, as one of the chiefs spoke. The wind carried his excited voice. "He's tellin' 'em it's goin' to be easy, Lieutenant," said the sergeant. "They got good carbines, he says, and good medicine, and seven hundred horses are waitin' for 'em and we got plenty of good carbines just waitin' for 'em to lug home." As the chief spoke they could make him out: he seemed elderly and a bit plump. The scalps fluttered on the lances in the wind, and the magpie feathers that hung from some of the buffalo horn headdresses turned and twisted so that the sun caught their iridescence and turned their purple into sudden green and gold.

"This is not going to be a picnic, Sergeant," said Lt. Stowe.

"No, sir."

"I thought Cross was doing us a favor when he tipped them off about our movements, but apparently he's been selling—or maybe even giving—carbines to the whole tribe."

"My God," said the sergeant, and he pointed. The silvery barrels of the carbines flashed as the Comanches pulled them from camouflaged saddle scabbards.

"Well, Sergeant, let's at least make a good fight of it. But if I'd known about this . . ." He turned to Lt. Wynn and asked, "How do you feel?"

Wynn's mouth was wide open as he watched.

"The truth?" he asked.

"The truth."

Lt. Wynn said, slowly, "I feel like I got a mouthful of cold peanut butter and I see the little blue and pink and green speckles, the kind that shines in a rooster's tail. Did you ever feel that way, Sam?"

"First time, yes. Also every other time it's about to start. But once it starts you forget that—here they come!"

But it was only a charge to put breath into their ponies, and the riders caught them up just out of range so shortly that several of them slid on their haunches. One of the youngest warriors sat there, fuming and anxious to win coup. Suddenly he turned to his companions, and said, "I, Haysoos, will ride against them alone and stampede their herd." His friend said, "You are crazy." Several other warriors heard him and laughed. Haysoos swung his pony's head around and pushed his way through the massed warriors. Still no one believed him, and several warriors said, "Stay here, crazy boy!" Haysoos walked his pony, paying no attention to their laughter, till he was free of them all.

He bent down and gathered a lot of dried grass. He tied it all together and attached a long rope to the bundle. Then he mounted, turned around, stood in his stirrups, waved once, and set off at a trot.

He forced his pony into the river and crossed it, still out of effective carbine range. When he had reached shore he lit his bundle. At this point the men, following orders, began firing at him.

He began to trot, then canter, then, as he neared the hill, to gallop. The flaming grass bounced and skidded behind him as he rode in a wide arc. To make himself lighter and enable his pony to run faster he dropped his shield. Most of the troopers thought for a moment he had accidentally dropped it or that he had been shot.

He forced his pony into a hard gallop. The grass touched off every dried patch it landed in, and the bone-dry stalks flared up in puffs of flame that immediately turned into puffs of smoke. Haysoos slipped an ankle into a horsehair loop that had been braided into the cantle of his saddle. He slung himself down on the far side of the pony so that all the target the troopers could fire at was his head.

Now the bullets were coming at him heavily. There was not enough grass to support a fire of any size, and the blazes that he had started were burning themselves out, not finding enough fuel to support a fire of real proportions. He saw it was useless, and rode back over the river, zigzagging as he went. He had been under fire for about three minutes.

Two bullets had hit Haysoos and one had carried away the lobe of his left ear. Another had sliced open his leggings and bruised the skin but had not drawn blood. Touch the Clouds greeted him as he galloped up and said, "This man now has a new name! I name him 'The Man Who Would Not Listen'!" Everyone shouted and Haysoos put a hand to his ear. It was bleeding badly, but he did not care. An older warrior, Grey Wolf, came up to him and said, "I have four war ponies—I want you to take any one you want and keep it!"

Now the warriors were excited. They milled around and did not listen to the older men. Suddenly three war chiefs pushed to the front and said, "Now! Now!" They pulled the rest after them and within a few seconds the charge had begun. Some of the raiders were painted yellow and wore the buffalo horns; others had the full war bonnet and were painted grey with horizontal white slashes on their forearms; still others, with only two or three feathers in their hair, had slashed their faces with crimson till they looked like masks. They came on in line of battle. This became a great V-formation. From the wings of the V there fanned out an irregular line of swirling warriors who began to move in circles, making swift extensions to the right and left at full gallop. There was no point in firing yet because of the distance and the erratic behavior of the ponies.

As the Comanches neared they began to move clockwise until an enormous wheel took shape. Slowly the wheel began to contract as the warriors shouted, "Yahooooo! Yaaaaaaaaa-hoooooo!"

The Comanches began firing. One bullet hit a wagon mule in the hindquarters; he began bucking, kicking up his legs, and drumming his heels against the side of the wagon to which he was tied. "That mule is changin' ends faster'n a woman can change her mind," said the sergeant.

"Hold your fire!" yelled the lieutenant. When the Comanches were within fifty yards he gave the order to fire at will. The sergeant fired at a war-bonneted head that had slung itself on the far side of its pony. A feather suddenly shot up from the bonnet and fluttered behind to the ground, shot in two. "Damn you!" said the sergeant, "if I can't kill you, I'll pluck you!"

The mingled voices of the officers and the sergeant rose and fell: "Steady there, you!"

"Take your proper intervals!"

"It isn't bleeding bad; you can walk to the first-aid wagon."

"Damn it, Reilly, are you firing at the Rockies?"

"Fire at the bonnets! Get the chiefs first!"

Three of the Comanche ponies trotted out of the circle with empty saddles. One of the ponies dragged his rider, who had been shot through the lungs, until two other warriors sat him back on his saddle, and, supporting him between them, trotted out of range. His war bonnet had been scraped off his head by a low clump of sagebrush; it hung there, its scarlet, yellow, black and white feathers glowing brilliantly among the brown withered branches. Another warrior galloped through a sudden fusillade, and, although shot in the leg, leaned down and snatched up the bonnet at full gallop. It fluttered behind him as he brought it to the ridge.

Many of the wounds suffered by the troopers were in the head or shoulders, because this was all that was exposed. But four men had died already, their skulls blown open by the heavy and accurate fire. "It's them new carbines," said the sergeant. "I tell you, Lieutenant, Cross musta given them plenty ammunition for practice. I never saw such good shootin' from them before this."

Firing began back of them, along the willow-edged river. Several warriors had swum across, protected by their horses' flanks, and were shooting at the men posted by the river banks. Others, from across the river, poured such a heavy fire into the willows that several of the guards were shot. This barrier removed, many warriors swarmed across the river, and sheltered among the willows, fired upward at the exposed troopers.

"Wynn!" said Lt. Stowe, "take ten men with you and see what you can do down there."

The damage was getting worse up in the rifle pits. Many men were shot in the back or hips, and whenever they tried to shoot down into the willows, the herd would be in the way.

One of the men suddenly stood up. An arrow, loosed by one of the youngest warriors who still could not afford a carbine, had gone completely through him, just under the ribs. It stuck out on both sides. He was moaning and trying to break off the dripping arrowhead and cutting his hand on the iron barb, heedless of the target he made. Just as Christie said, "Pull him down!" he was shot in the chest and collapsed.

Lt. Stowe looked down the slope at the river. From time to time he fired at the scalp locks braided with white otter fur or red flannel moving among the thick growth. Once he fired at a scalp that had four tiny silver bells braided into the scalp lock, and the wearer fell among the slender yellow branches of the young willows. Lt. Stowe saw that Wynn was having trouble. One of the chiefs had come across the river by holding on to the tail of his swimming horse, and reaching shore, mounted and splashed along the shallows till he came to where Wynn was directing the firing. He had come at him from the rear, and Wynn, because of the noise of the firing, yelling, and neighing of the horses, had not heard him. At the last second he turned, finally aware, and saw a lance driving down at him. He lifted a hand to deflect it, and the warrior's horse knocked him on his back in the warm shallow water. The Comanche made one more try with his lance; Wynn parried it once again as he struggled to get to his knees and pull his Colt. He fired twice at the warrior's heart. The Comanche slid off his pony and lay dead on his face in the water while the pony trotted off, sniffed at the herd, and then waded in and swam across the river.

Wynn's hand was sliced open where he had gripped the lance head. He stood, trembling, looking at the current carrying the bonnet of the dead chief downstream. It swirled around and around, and one of the warriors swam out to get it. Wynn shot him and he slid under in a sudden convulsive jerk. Some bloody froth came to the surface and mingled with the bonnet.

The death of the chief made most of the warriors hesitate. The firing from the men in the rifle pits was becoming more accurate as the lieutenant and the sergeant and the corporals yelled at them to take their time as they squeezed the triggers, and the guards posted among the willows were shooting better. The better marksmen were picking off the warriors across the river, and two more chiefs, picked out by their bonnets, were killed.

The slope in front of the pits was littered with dead Comanches. Again and again two or three warriors would break out of the revolving circle and charge the slope, firing as they came, and half or three-quarters of the way up they would drop. One warrior reached the top of the slope before he was killed, and Sgt. Christie wriggled out of his pit, slid down ten feet, picked up the carbine, and slid back, bullets making the sand spurt all around him. He and the lieutenant looked at the carbine.

"Latest model," said the lieutenant.

"Better'n ours. Cross is gun-runnin' in a big way." said Christie.

"But how does he get them to the Comanches?"

"Maybe through the Cheyenne country. Maybe he gets 'em at Omaha and takes 'em along the Platte with the emigrant wagons and then cuts down into Comanche country. Or maybe he comes up from Big Springs with 'em stuck in barrels labelled flour. I seen that before. He goes away for two-three weeks at a time. Says he has to go to San Antonio or up to St. Louis to get supplies. It ain't far from St. Louis to Omaha, either. And before he come out to be agent no more than two or three out of ten braves would have guns. Now I bet nine out of ten got 'em and they sure know how to handle 'em. Before Cross came all the guns they'd have would be old ones, from before the war, and a lot of 'em would be muskets from the Mexican War. Well, no use cryin'. By the way, Lieutenant, McDonald's men are doing all right. They've got some wounded, too.''

The firing had stopped for a few minutes: the Comanches were reforming, and mounting fresh ponies that the younger boys were bringing up, or snatching a few bites of pemmican. The lieutenant crawled from pit to pit, checking the ammunition, and then he slid down the slope, saw that Beth was all right, and walked among the wounded. Wynn was there, getting his hand bandaged. "My first," he said, awed and proud.

The herd had calmed down somewhat. Lt. Stowe went back up the slope at a zigzag run; two shots from across the river missed him. A drum began beating out of carbine range, somewhere behind the massed warriors.

It was going to be a mass charge. They began slowly at first; as they neared the slope they changed to a hard gallop, hoping that their momentum would carry them into the pits. The firing was very heavy from both sides, and from a hundred yards the Comanches began dropping; the sand spurted up all around the sides of the pits, and some of the men were temporarily blinded by sand grains being driven into their eyes.

This time the charge carried them almost to the rim of the hill, but the damage was so severe among them that they could not do any more. It was their last charge, and as they fell back, firing, some of the warriors picked up the carbines dropped by the dead and wounded. They withdrew out of range, still firing. Two of the troopers were reckless enough to stand up and yell, and one of them was shot in the temple and died immediately.

The warriors along the river swam back with their horses, and the soldiers kept up a deadly fire into the water. In a few minutes all the Comanches had withdrawn, gathering together far upstream, crossing it, and riding behind the distant ridge where their ponies waited.

Lt. Wynn asked, "Shall I go after them?" Lt. Stowe looked at the slope filled with the dead, the dead on the plain below, the brown bodies facedown among the yellow willows staining the river, the bodies sprawled across the far shore, the bodies in the pits, and the dying troopers moaning among the wagons or breathing heavily through grey lips as they lay in shock.

"No," he said. "We're too chewed up. If we follow them they'll jump us from good defensive positions on the ridge. We've done enough for this afternoon."

Lt. Stowe walked among the warriors who were sprawled on the slope. "Careful, Lieutenant!" said Sgt. Christie, following with his drawn Colt, "one of 'em might be playin' dead."

Lt. Stowe pulled his Colt and walked with it drawn. "I'm looking for one that's still alive," he said. "I want a confession if I can get it. I want one to say where he got the carbines."

They turned over several bodies. Three of the wounded would not talk, and one was unconscious. The fifth one was badly wounded in the chest, and in great pain, but conscious. He was lying on his carbine and made a move to lift it when he saw the whites bending over him, but the sergeant easily pulled it out from under him. He looked up at them, panting, and blood trickled out of his mouth and the big hole in his chest.

Lt. Stowe looked down at him. He called out for McDonald to come with paper and a pencil. The Comanche looked up. He knew he was going to die soon.

"Where did you get the carbine?" asked Christie.

The Comanche smiled. "A white man," he said. "A white man who wants to see you soldiers killed. We do not like him and he wants too much for the guns but now we have all we want. They are good carbines!''

"What does he look like?"

"He is bald and said we should not know his name, but I have seen him at Fort Brill. He is the new agent."

"Do you know you are dying?"

"I know."

"What is your name?"

"Red Bull."

"Do you like the new agent?"

"We will kill him the next time we see him. We are to meet him by Big Springs the next moon. We will give him buffalo hides and he will give us more guns and ammunition and then we will kill him."

"Why?"

"We will have enough guns then. If we kill him we will take back our buffalo hides and we will have his gun also."

"McDonald," said Lt. Stowe, "write down what he just said." Then he turned to the Comanche and asked, "Why do you tell me this?"

"We were to kill him but I see my friends are dead. If I tell you, you will kill him." His mouth filled with blood.

"Hurry up, McDonald!" said the lieutenant.

"All done," said McDonald.

"Make your mark here," said Lt. Stowe, and the Comanche did so. Lt. Stowe wrote "Red Bull, his mark," and Lt. Wynn, writing awkwardly with his bandaged hand, Beth, who had come up, the lieutenants and Sgt. Christie, signed as witnesses. Under Christie's signature the lieutenant had him write, "I swear that I have faithfully translated what Red Bull said."

Red Bull died soon after. It took a few hours to bury the dead. There was no more grass, and they had to move on. In that place, by the bend of the river, whose name they did not even know, they left forty-seven of their own men and over a hundred Comanches. McDonald had four dead and four wounded.

The rest of the day there were no more signal smokes. They made a dry camp. The wounded were in great pain because of the motion of the wagons, and the horses were restless with hunger. The next day was worse, and late that afternoon the two men on point began making the discovery sign: riding rapidly in circles. Then one of them galloped back and called out, "Come see this, Lieutenant!"

Lt. Stowe galloped past the herd and up to the other man on point, who sat his horse, pointing below.

From the crest of the dry, rock-strewn ridge, they looked down into a green valley that ran ten miles long and three miles wide. Through the middle of the valley a stream of clear water lazed through groves of willow and wild plum. On the gentle slopes along the bottom meadows grazed deer, antelope, and wild horses, and under the interlocking branches of the oaks scattered over the valley floor flocks of wild turkeys were feeding on the acorns. A few late bumblebees droned over the last fall flowers, and in the warm sky, immensely high, was the sound of the wind. A single bird was singing somewhere in the wild plum trees.

FIFTEEN

"Hold everyone here till we come back," said Lt. Stowe. "Don't let anyone shoot at the game yet. Come on, Sergeant. Let's go down into the valley for a scout."

The two men rode slowly into the valley, past a clump of persimmons that the first frost had ripened into fat tight green globes. High up in one of the persimmon trees a fat little possum stared at the riders, astonished.

Then came a grove of pecans; on the farther side grazed two deer. When they heard the crunch of the pecans under the horses' hooves, they lifted their antlered heads and stared, like the possum. They then lowered their heads again. "Ride at 'em slow, Lieutenant," said the sergeant. They did so, and the deer let them get within thirty feet before they moved.

They rode along the banks of the stream for a while. A few great green frogs sat on lily pads and gazed at them, and five antelope wandered out from a dense stand of cedar growing up on the valley slopes and looked at them, their jaws moving slowly. "Wanna see five white rear ends all at once?" asked the sergeant. He clapped his hands and his prediction came true; the antelope bounded in great leaps across the meadow.

They reined in and ate persimmons. "I tell you one thing, Lieutenant," said the sergeant, "ain't no one hunted this valley yet. I ain't seen old campfires, and if we shoot careful it'll be a while before they get scared of us."

They pulled out their carbines and waited till two antelope had drifted deep enough under the oaks so as not to be seen by the others.

"Now," said the lieutenant, and they squeezed their triggers. Both antelope staggered a few feet, then collapsed. The whole valley awoke with the sound of the shots. A few wild turkeys ran hard out from under the oaks and took flight to the valley below where they stuck their long necks into the grass, trembling.

The men slung the game across their saddles and turned back to rejoin the others. On the way back the lieutenant stopped under a persimmon, stood in his stirrups, and filled his saddle bag with persimmons.

"Them persimmons!" said the sergeant, munching. "Eat one and you'll hunt up the creek and eat fifty. See that possum up in the tree havin' a high ol' time for hisself?"

When McDonald saw the antelope he could hardly restrain himself. When he heard of the sweet water and the wild turkey, he said, "Lieutenant, you're in charge like we agreed, but how about restin' up for three-four days?"

Lt. Stowe was watching the cook start to skin the antelope. "I'm for it," he said.

McDonald was exuberant. The exhausted and wounded men ate and went to sleep early. The night was cool and foggy. The next day was warm and pleasant after a clear and cloudless dawn, and the day after that the same. The men hunted or sun-bathed or fished in the clear water for the speckled trout.

The wounded were getting better with the good food and the rest, the warm days and cool nights. Wynn's hand had healed enough so that he could handle his carbine again on hunts for vension. The horses' ribs were fleshing out with the excellent grass. Lt. Stowe looked at them grazing. "Another two days," he remarked, "and we'll be fit for travel."

The men still kept guard, but everyone felt that an attack was unlikely: the Comanches had taken such a beating that they could not afford to lose any more warriors, and the valley itself showed no signs of ever being hunted.

One morning before sunrise Beth and Lt. Stowe rode out. The great yellow glow of Venus swiftly turned into a small topaz, and as the sun topped the horizon she slowly became smaller and smaller until she was the same size as the other stars; then all of them merged into the sky and it was full day.

They rode slowly for an hour, deeper into the valley. The day had burned away some low-lying fog that had drifted over the willows and Beth unbuttoned her jacket. They topped a rise; before them was a tiny valley three hundred feet long, fifty feet wide, and flat as a floor before its side sloped steeply upward. Its high sides had kept it out of the winds and more flowers were there than anywhere else in the valley. They rode down to the bottom, dismounted among waist-high purple asters and let the reins hang; their horses began to graze. The great sky of the prairie suddenly shrank to their own personal sky.

Beth sat among the asters and said, "I'll miss it here in green-up time. That's when the bluebonnets come up in the meadows back at the Fort. And I'll feel like an idiot in Washington. I don't even know how to waltz. And when I dine out—with all those folks—" She sighed.

The lieutenant held out his big and calloused hands. "Can you imagine these things holding the right fork? It took four years at the Point. Was it Wynn who told me there's a town in Maryland named after your family? The only thing named after my family are the women we bring home to Cherry Valley. That's a lot to ask of anyone who's been brought up Army—and who's had a town named after her great-great-grandfather.''

He stood up. "I think we ought to ride back."

"Great-grandfather," she said. "You're the biggest snob I've ever met."

He set his jaw and waited. Beth got up and the two of them mounted and rode out of the valley.

They ate trout for supper; and afterwards one of McDonald's men brought out his harmonica and Beth sang "Shenandoah" as the swift dusk filled the valley. With the darkness came the usual heavy fog rolling up from the stream.

Many of the men edged closer as Beth sang. Sgt. Christie leaned across, took the harmonica, wiped it, and began to play "The Girl I Left Behind Me." Beth sang this one, too, looking down at Lt. Stowe, who was sitting cross-legged on the ground. Some of the guard drifted nearer to listen, huddled in their blankets. The three men guarding the horses rode nearer, and lit cigarettes. Then the cowpuncher took back his harmonica, wiped it carefully, grinned, and began to play "Oh Susanna."

He usually played well, and when he suddenly hit a sour chord, Lt. Stowe, surprised, turned to look at him. He had dropped his harmonica, and his two hands were trying to break the head off the war arrow that had come clean through his throat from behind. Two more arrows just missed Lt. Stowe's head and stuck, quivering, into the water keg. He stood up and started to run for his saddle, where the carbine lay in its scabbard. He had gone ten feet when an arrow went through his left thigh. He fell, and started to crawl towards the the saddle, but a lasso dropped around him and was pulled tight. He was helpless. Sgt. Christie was one of the few wearing a Colt; as he went for it a thrown war club knocked him unconscious. Beth made a try for her carbine, but a Comanche had come into her wagon from the rear and as her hand reached for her carbine he grabbed it and pulled her inside. She started to kick, but another warrior climbed in through the front of the wagon and lashed her hands behind her with rawhide thong.

McDonald had been lying in his blanket half-asleep. He threw it back and was still lying on one elbow when a warrior drove a lance through him. He screamed and tried to move, but the force of the thrust had sent the blade a foot into the ground. All he could do was wriggle a bit on the end of the blade. Lt. Wynn had been pinioned by three warriors; he was being bound with rawhide thongs.

So expert had been the Comanche approach through the fog that only a few shots had been fired by the escort or McDonald's men. The war party consisted of over a hundred warriors, and almost all the dead had three arrows in them. There was some quarreling about the scalps, but this was quickly stopped by the war chief, a short heavy-set man named Kicking Bird, who was Yellow Bird's father.

This war party had few carbines, unlike the other party that had attacked at the bend of the river. But Kicking Bird, like the other chief, had been told by Cross of the horse herd. He had picked up Stowe's trail two days before, and had followed him into the valley. Kicking Bird held Lt. Stowe responsible for the death of his son, and he was very pleased that Stowe had been taken alive.

Kicking Bird was unusually old and fat for a war chief; but he was famous and had never returned with his face painted black and his pony's tail shaved.

Kicking Bird stood looking down impassively at the prisoners. Lt. Stowe was having his wrists bound with far more force than was necessary. The shaft of the war arrow was turning red as Lt. Stowe's blood oozed down the grooves cut along the shaft. "Break it," said Kicking Bird.

Someone knelt and broke the shaft.

Kicking Bird ordered more logs thrown on the fire. One of the younger warriors had ridden back over the ridge where their ponies and provisions had been hidden during the raid; he came cantering back and handed Kicking Bird his buffalo robe. The chief put it around him since the night was steadily growing more and more chilly. The fire blazed up.

Kicking Bird said, in Comanche, "I want the officers from Fort Brill and the daughter of Major Welles. I recognize her. I see no reason to keep the others. We can kill them now."

The Fox, who was carefully wrapping three scalps in a buckskin bag, said, angrily, "I think we should kill all the prisoners now. They are not all your prisoners. We will not kill the woman if you wish."

Another warrior said, "I wish to do as Kicking Bird orders. He has led us well up to now. Some of the men will die well, and will take too long to die here; we will lose too much time. We should kill them at the camp."

Someone rode up with Kicking Bird's riding horse, a pinto striped with red paint like a zebra. A buckskin pouch hung from the saddle horn. Kicking Bird touched it gently; his eyes filled with tears. The pouch held the bones of Yellow Bird, his son. "I wish to go to our camp," he said.

He mounted his horse and pulled his robe about him. In grief for his son he had cut off his little finger of the left hand at the first joint; he had left no flaps of flesh, and as a result the wound had healed leaving half an inch of bone sticking out.

He bent over the buckskin bag on his saddle and mumbled something. Sgt. Christie was conscious now, blood running down his head from the laceration where he had been struck with the war club. He turned his head and said, "Lieutenant, you all right?"

"My leg hurts. Not too bad."

"Beth?"

"All right," she said.

Lt. Wynn, Wheaton and Schweizer were all unhurt. Lt. Stowe said, "I guess we're the only ones alive."

Sergeant Christie said, "They want to make an example of Fort Brill, I bet."

Horses were brought up; the prisoners were placed astride, and their ankles viciously lashed together. A deerskin bag with a hole cut at the mouth and nose for air was jammed over Beth's head, and at a sharp trot the war party headed for the western end of the valley. As they passed McDonald, Kicking Bird halted and looked down. McDonald still moved. Kicking Bird grunted and pulled out his lance and went on. As the prisoners rode by they could hear him moaning.

The captured herd was to follow as soon as there was enough light.

"How is it we don't get masks, too?" asked Lt. Wynn.

The sergeant was silent. "Yes, Sergeant?" Wynn persisted.

Beth was out of hearing. "They want to trade her, I guess," said the sergeant. "So they don't want her to recognize the trail and maybe lead back a command this way. But we ain't comin' back. So they don't care if we see where we're goin'."

The lieutenant could hear the Comanches laughing. They had no casualties this time; had taken many prisoners, one of whom should bring them rifles and horses. Almost everyone had counted coup, and each warrior was to receive at least five horses and his share of the booty.

The temporary ownership of the woman was a problem, but that would be settled three days to the northeast. As for the present, they had to move, and quickly: they did not know if another patrol were following or not.

SIXTEEN

They rode till sunrise. It was a hard night: frequently the ponies stopped to take a bite of grass and the prisoners would pitch forward; then as suddenly the ponies would start off at a sharp trot and the prisoners would fall backward. Several times they were unable to hold themselves erect by the pressure of their thighs, and they would roll over and lie, helpless, head downward under their horses' bellies. Then the horses stopped and began eating until one of the warriors rode alongside and pulled them upright again.

At sunrise they stopped. They were taken off, and their hands tied in front of them so that they could eat. This was the procedure followed at every meal. A worn-out horse was then killed by having its throat cut. A small fire was made and the horseflesh hastily broiled; a sizzling and bloody chunk was hacked off and tossed at each prisoner in turn.

It became obvious that the Comanches were playing a game. The purpose was to make the hot fat-smeared meat land on their bare faces, necks, or arms. Whenever the thrower was successful, a shout of laughter went up. Wynn was hit three times on the face, and through his stubble his face was beginning to blister. Beth's neck was burned; Wheaton and Schweizer were each burned several times. Lt. Stowe had turned his head quickly when he saw the meat thrown at him—he was hit under his right ear.

His leg wound was beginning to swell. The broken shaft was sticking out. An infected leg would spoil the torture to which he was to be subjected: the stronger a man was the longer he would last under torture. Kicking Bird gave a brief order. A young warrrior rode off and was back within ten minutes with the bark of the slippery elm.

In the meantime another warrior had knelt down and made a deep cut with his knife along the shaft and down to the arrowhead. The lieutenant brought his rawhide thong up to his mouth and bit it as the Comanche worked the arrowhead loose and into the incision and pulled upwards on the splintered shaft. The arrowhead slid out, followed by upwelling of blood. The Comanche waited a few moments. Then he squeezed the flesh surrounding the wound. Lt. Stowe gasped. Beth was biting her lip. The Comanche placed the elm bark on top of the wound, and bound it in place with a strip of red calico he had taken from his saddle pouch.

Then they were set once more on their horses, their legs bound under them, and once more the march began up into Comanche territory. Once in a while the trail led to valleys where there was a growth of trees. Unable to protect themselves from the low branches the prisoners would be struck on the face, head, and shoulders.

When they stopped at noon for the usual meal of almost raw horsemeat, they looked at one another. Lt. Stowe had been the first in line, so he looked the worst, as if he had been badly beaten. One eye was puffed, his left cheek was discolored, and a lump on his forehead had started to swell.

Beth was riding third in line, and was not so bad—all she had were a few welts where some of the smaller branches bent aside by Sgt. Christie had whipped back.

She refused to eat the horsemeat. Sgt. Christie said, "You better eat. You got to be strong for whatever happens. Just grit your teeth, Miss Welles, and swaller." At first it was hard for her, but toward the end of the meal she was getting the chunks of meat down without too much trouble.

Then they were placed astride their horses once more, the ankle thongs made fast again. The pressure forced Lt. Stowe's thigh hard against the side of his horse; Beth saw him wince before the mask was slipped over her head. They rode all afternoon, smashed and whipped on the face, head and shoulders whenever they came near a tree-lined stream.

Toward sunset the scouts found a good camp: a high hill with water from a spring nearby. The war party rounded the hill, climbed it, and halted near the top, but on the side opposite to that whence they had come. Sentries were posted on the side of the hill from where possible pursuit might come.

Once more they ate. Then four stakes were driven into the ground for each prisoner. They were placed face upward, spread-eagled, and each wrist and ankle was made fast to a stake. Then two more stakes were driven in, one on each side of their throats, and a rawhide strap passed between the stakes, so that they could not lift their heads.

In this position they passed the night. In the beginning it was hard to sleep because of the lack of blankets, the damp ground, the aches, and the throbbing from being beaten in the face by the trees. But so great was their exhaustion that they fell asleep in five and ten-minute snatches—all except Lt. Stowe and Lt. Wynn. The former could not sleep because of his leg, and Wynn could not because he had developed a bad cough during the day.

Toward morning Sgt. Christie looked at Beth; she was

asleep. He turned his head toward Lt. Stowe and whispered, "Lieutenant, remember when we was ridin' back from San Anselmo and you looked at your knuckles and you figured you musta hit some one good, particularly one of those cowpunchers from the Rocking Horse?"

The lieutenant said he remembered.

"You felt pretty good about that?"

The lieutenant said, yes, he did.

"Well, lemme tell you the truth, Lieutenant—you was so awful blind you got on your knees and swung hard as you could at the bar. That's who you hit—the bar. I was never gonna tell you, Lieutenant, but you get me so mad the way you behave with Beth."

The lieutenant whispered back, "Keep out of this. Nobody weighing two hundred pounds can play Cupid."

The sergeant paid no attention. "And Kitty Burton," he said. "Kitty Burton! She said she wanted to see Kitty Burton before she went east! Lemme tell you about *that*. Their daddies used to be captains together at the same fort and the two girls hated one another somethin' awful—I was always pullin' 'em apart by their braids. She wanted to see Kitty Burton as much as she wants to get bit by a scorpion. If you can't still figure why she rode all the way alone to Buffalo Bone Ford—I never thought I'd serve under such a dumb lieutenant. And that's all I have to say."

The lieutenant was quiet.

"What am I now," asked the sergeant, "a private?"

"No," said the lieutenant, so quietly the sergeant could barely hear him.

Beth said, "Boo, be quiet."

"How you feelin'?" asked the sergeant.

"All right, I guess."

"They're gonna trade you for rifles and horses, honey," said Boo, "so don't worry."

"That's what you think," she said, "but I know better. And so do you. You know what Dad will do. He wouldn't give them a single rifle or horse. He'd ride alone into their camp and fight them all. But not a rifle or a pony."

Boo was silent. "So," Beth went on, "we're all in the same mess."

"How you feelin', Wheaton?" asked Lt. Stowe.

"All right."

"You, Schweizer?"

"All right, Lieutenant."

"Wynn?"

"All right."

The lieutenant went on. "I want all you men to eat all you can and sleep all you can. Sooner or later there may come a chance to high-tail it and I don't want anyone to drop off along the way. We can't make it tonight—I can't walk, and they're watching too carefully. But sooner or later they're going to get too confident."

They were silent and shivering as they listened.

Somehow they slept a little. But for Lt. Stowe sleep was impossible because of his leg. Lt. Wynn couldn't sleep because he found it too hard to breathe easily. Toward morning Venus rose, butter-yellow and unbelievable as ever. The lieutenant watched that one great star hanging in the honeyed air, then turned his head sideward under his neck thong and his eyes met Beth's. She smiled. Her hair was tangled with dried leaves and burrs and her upper lip was puffy and discolored and her neck was beginning to blister where the horsemeat had been thrown.

That day and night it was the same story—run under trees, pelted with hot horseflesh, and staked down at night. It rained hard that afternoon and the Comanches were irritated as they always were when it rained on a war or hunting party: their trail would be easy to follow in the damp soil.

Kicking Bird rode huddled under his buffalo robe. His son's bones banged gently together in their buckskin bag. One hand held the robe together; this was the hand whose little finger ended in an inch-long spike of white bone.

Toward the end of the afternoon, Lt. Wynn's cough got worse. When a particularly bad fit came his body twisted in a desperate attempt to drive more air into his lungs. Kicking Bird looked at him, annoyed. Lt. Wynn had pneumonia and his back and sides hurt, and after a violent fit of coughing and gasping Kicking Bird said, "I do not like this. He will make too much noise. There are Osage war parties out."

Then he added, without passion, "Kill him. I claim his scalp." The war party stopped, and in the stillness Beth heard the two horses walking up to the lieutenant.

Two arrows suddenly feathered his side; Beth trembled as she heard the twang of the bowstrings and the agonized "Ahhhhhh" of the lieutenant. The two bowstrings twanged again and two more bunches of turkey feathers appeared beside the first two. Wynn began twisting and he suddenly pitched sideward and hung suspended under his horse's belly. Once more the bowstrings twanged. His horse began to graze. He choked and tried to say something. Then he sobbed once and died.

A Comanche rode up and cut his ankle thongs. He dropped to the ground. The Comanche dismounted, made an incision the size of a silver dollar in the center of the blonde hair. Then he placed a muddy moccasin on the lieutenant's shoulder and pulled. The scalp came off with a pop! The Comanche handed it to Kicking Bird, who wrapped it in some calico he had removed from his saddle pouch and carefully inserted it. Then the Comanche took off the saddle and bridle from the lieutenant's horse, and slapped it on the rump; the horse cantered off to join the herd.

The rain let up an hour later. The Comanches forced their horses on faster; they did not mind pushing them. They were only a day's march from their village where there was plenty of good grass. Supper that night was quickly made and quickly eaten as if they could not wait to get to sleep and start riding once more with the sunrise.

The prisoners could not sleep. Their clothes were damp, it was much colder than the night before, and Wynn's savage death had angered them.

The warriors were too excited to sleep, but Kicking Bird, wrapping himself in his robe, lay down to sleep. One of the warriors who claimed Beth squatted beside her, pulled her head around by her braids, and stared at her. Then he placed one hand on her breast. She spat at him. He jerked his head back, furious, and went for his knife. Several of the warriors laughed, and another warrior who claimed her placed his hand on his knife hilt.

Kicking Bird woke up, and said, "Do not touch her, either of you! We shall talk about this tomorrow. If there is more fighting over her I shall kill her and neither of you shall have anything. Go and sleep!" The warrior walked away sullenly, wiping his face. There was laughter, and Kicking Bird said, "Enough!"

The morning came at last, clear and cold. A little before noon the war party stopped to send smoke signals. They ate some pemmican and each warrior took a handful of grass and rubbed it down his best war pony: he wished it to look clean and fresh when they entered the village. Then they rode on for two more hours through country that gradually became more and more wooded.

Far across a broad valley they saw a mass of tepees clustered inside a huge grove of cottonwoods. The trees grew on one side of the broad river that flowed swiftly in a smother of green foam from the foothills of the Rockies. A figure on horseback was galloping out to meet them.

As it neared the war party the lieutenant could see it was an old woman riding beautifully with a long lance balanced across her horse's withers. The party halted and waited for her. Her son was one of the youngest warriors; it was his first war party.

When she saw him she gave no sign of recognition. She said to Kicking Bird, "Did my son count coup?"

Kicking Bird said, "He has taken two scalps. He has counted coup four times."

She said, "I feel glad as the ponies do when the first grass starts at the beginning of the year." Her son rode up and tied his two scalps to the lance. One of them had long grey hair. Several of the other warriors smiled at her, and four of them rode up, and, saying, "I give you my scalps to carry in," tied them to the lance.

She held the lance aloft with both hands, guiding her pony with the pressure of her knees. The village was laid out in the form of a square, as far as the trees among which the tepees were pitched would allow. As they rode down between streets formed by two irregular lines of trees they were surrounded by jumping and jubilant children and barking dogs. In front of a few tepees the lieutenant noticed tripods made out of three lances tied together at the top; shields were hung from them in the sun for good medicine. All the tepee entrances faced east toward the rising sun.

One by one the warriors dropped off—they were going home to take their hoops of willow and to start curing their scalps so they would be at least partly ready for the scalp dance. With their proud younger brothers and sisters or nephews sitting behind them other warriors rode back to the herd to claim their share of the captured horses.

Kicking Bird stopped in front of a large tepee; surrounding it were four smaller ones. Each of these belonged to one of his four wives, all of whom, plump and old, stood waiting and smiling. He dismounted heavily, unhooked the buckskin bag with the bones of Yellow Bird and gave it to the oldest squaw, who was Yellow Bird's mother. She unclasped her folded hands and took it into Kicking Bird's tepee.

He gave several brief orders. The prisoners' ankle thongs were removed and they were pulled off their horses. The lashings had been so tight that it was hard for them to walk. Lt. Stowe limped; one of the warriors shoved him impatiently. His arms were still bound behind him and there was no way to break the fall. He took it on his face and left shoulder. He slowly got to his knees and looked for three seconds at the man who had shoved him. It was a warrior with a scarred face under a buffalo horn headdress.

Then he got painfully to his feet and walked into the tepee, followed by the others. It was dark at first, but after a while they got used to it. Light came in through the eastern opening, which was simply a buffalo robe, tied back in good weather, and in bad weighted down with a stone or log. More light poured down through the smoke hole at the apex of the tepee. The floor was made of several layers of buffalo hides and scattered along the lower tepee walls and hanging from the lodge poles were buckskin bags filled with the belongings of a successful war chief—arrows, bows, buckskin shirts and leggings, moccasins, scalps, saddles, and buffalo robes; not much else. For the wealth of a chief was measured in horses, and of these, Kicking Bird owned a hundred and sixty. He had taken them from points along a great arc that swung from the Platte down to the mountains of southern Durango—from Mexicans, cowpunchers, buffalo hunters, homesteaders, ranchers, cavalrymen, miners; and the Osage, the Sioux, the Arapaho, and the Cheyenne.

One of the wives made a tripod out of three lances and hung his shield, which bore horses' tails on the front, the sign of a great raider. Two other wives made food. They broiled some buffalo meat between two logs in front of the tepee. When it was ready one of them took a four foot stick sharpened at both ends, stuck one end in the meat, and the other end into the ground, from where the buffalo robe floor had been temporarily pulled back.

As they ate, Kicking Bird came in with a boy of sixteen. "Well, I'll be goddammed, Lieutenant! Know who that is?" asked Boo.

The lieutenant didn't recognize him. "That's the brave

who tried to set fire to the grass." The sergeant looked at Haysoos in admiration.

"Take off their thongs," Kicking Bird said. As Haysoos was doing this, Kicking Bird walked to the entrance of the tepee and called, "I want three warriors with rifles." Three men dismounted and walked in. "Watch them," said Kicking Bird. They sat down on the other side of the tepee from the prisoners. "Feed them well," said Kicking Bird. "The men will need their strength tonight."

One squaw set out a bark dish full of boiled corn. To each she gave a piece of buffalo meat and a spoon made of buffalo horn.

When the lieutenant had finished eating he carefully bared his thigh and began unwrapping the calico bandage. Sgt. Christie crawled over to look at the wound. This brought him a bit nearer one of the guards. There was the click of a carbine being cocked, and the guard said, in Comanche, "Go back!" Christie looked at him, pretending he did not understand, and the warrior held up one hand, palm out, and made a pushing motion. It was the same scarred man who had pushed the lieutenant into the tepee.

The sergeant moved back. "I'm gonna have to deal with that one," he said softly.

Beth kept looking at Haysoos. The boy stared back, curiously. Then he noticed that the corn was gone from the dish. He threw it to one of the squaws, who left for more. When she brought it back, full, Haysoos took it and set it down among the prisoners.

Beth said, "He's no Comanche. He's got grey eyes."

"You speak English?" asked the sergeant. The boy looked at him blankly.

"Usted mexicano?"

The boy said proudly, *"Soy Comanche."*

"He's Mexican, all right," said the sergeant. "Haysoos! "That's J-e-s-u-s." He continued in Spanish, "How long have you been a prisoner?"

The boy, annoyed, said slowly, searching for half-for-gotten words, "I am not a prisoner. I am a Comanche."

"All right, you're a Comanche," said the sergeant. "How long have you been a Comanche?"

"Kicking Bird has been my father for—for—" He forgot the word for "years," and finally he said ". . . ten springs."

"Where are you from?"

"Oh, they took me from far away." He motioned to the south. "They came with the moon of the Comanches. It took us two more moons to come back. We raided some more and we took three more children from Mexico and one from Texas. But they were no good."

He was scornful. "They cried too much so they killed them. The one from Texas was very little, so they cut a hole under its chin and hung it from a broken branch and left it. I did not cry and they put me on my stomach and tied my hands and feet up in the air to two stakes and they put a heavy stone on my back all night. I did not cry and then they took off the stone and untied me and I tried to bite Yellow Bird and he laughed and Kicking Bird took me for his son."

Haysoos stood erect and proud.

Lt. Stowe asked, "Will he help?"

Sgt. Christie said glumly, "If you think he'll give us that knife, forget about it. The only way he'll give it to us will be in our ribs. He's dyin' for scalps. He's Comanche, all right."

It was rapidly growing dark. Haysoos made a fire in the tepee. He made no attempt at conversation with the prisoners, but sat with the warriors on the other side. The scar-faced one and Haysoos began to play a knuckle game, and the prisoners, warm and unbound at night for the first time, stretched out. The lieutenant's leg was not infected and was beginning to heal.

He took Beth's hand and kissed it. She smiled at him and kissed his hand, and they fell asleep; in the tepee the only sounds were the crackling of the small fire, the murmuring and sudden laughter of the knuckle-bone players. In the other tepees the warriors were preparing their scalps; those who were lucky enough to have scalps with long hair were oiling and combing them.

Suddenly the drums began.

SEVENTEEN

The four men were bound by the scarred warrior Bear Wolf, and Haysoos, and taken out. The moon was in the quarter with that furry white halo around it that meant rain; a few stars showed through the gaps in the low-racing clouds. High up above the tepees the topmost branches of the cottonwoods were stirring and thrashing in the wind. Underneath it was dark, but a faint glow showed through the smoke openings of several tepees; the others were dark. Near the river big fires had been lit and from them came the sound of the drums. The fires burned in the center of a flat meadow surrounded on three sides by the tepees; on the fourth flowed the river, swift and green. To one side of the fire sat four old men, drumming and shaking gourd rattles.

In the center of this area, near the fires, four sets of poles had been set up. Each pole was eight feet tall and the poles of each set were five feet apart. The men were stripped naked and placed between the poles. Their wrists and ankles were tied to the poles in such a way that they were suspended in air. Wheaton was trembling, and Lt.

Stowe's wound had opened again under the strain of his position. The blood was running down his leg and dripping slowly between his toes. Schweizer stared at the blood, fascinated. All the warriors of Kicking Bird's party were there.

One by one, to the sound of the banging drums and the rattles, they recited their coups. The Fox said, "I crawled within five feet of one of the men watching the horses. There was fog. Then three feet. He was holding a carbine in his hands; I came behind him and I took his neck in my elbow and I killed him with my knife. I took his scalp."

He held it aloft. "This is the truth!" The drums banged, the rattles shook, and the listeners clapped, stamped their feet and yelled the war whoop. Then another warrior came up and recited his coups. When they had all finished the warriors formed a single file and began to circle around the two sets of posts that held Wheaton and Schweizer. It was half a walk, half a shuffle. Each of the warriors held a sharp piece of flint in his hand.

Slowly the drums increased their beat, slowly the dancers increased their speed until drops of sweat began to appear on their bodies. Suddenly one of them lunged out of line and sliced with the flint at Schweizer's stomach. When the flint came away a red sheet slid down his abdomen. Another warrior raked his flint down Wheaton's left leg, from his hip to his knee.

None of the cuts were deep, but after ten minutes of being slashed, both men looked as if they had been dipped in red paint up to their necks. Wheaton kept repeating, "Oh, God. Oh, God. Oh, God . . ."

Schweizer was silent, but his eyes were filled with hatred, and finally, when a warrior dropped his flint and pulled a knife from his belt Schweizer said, "Goddam you!" and spat at him. The Comanche grabbed Schweizer's hair with one hand and with the other scalped him. He took most of the scalp and Schweizer's forehead slid down half an inch and became a wrinkled red sheet.

The blood poured into his eyes and blinded him; it ran into his mouth and he began to spit it out. He twisted his body, weeping with rage, spitting blood, and screaming, "Dirty rotten lousy Comanche!" He shook his head, trying to force the blood from his eyes, but more poured in. He tried tilting his head to one side to see better; he closed them for a moment, he tried squinting—this way he could see. He closed them for a moment. He opened them just in time to see a warrior coming at him with an uplifted tomahawk.

Wheaton was trembling uncontrollably. Suddenly he lost control of his sphincter muscles. The Fox looked at him, disgusted. He jerked his head; a warrior tomahawked him immediately. The dancers then swung toward Sergeant Christie and Lt. Stowe, yelling the war whoop, and suddenly the drums stopped. Two warriors walked toward them with their knives drawn. The two men set their teeth, and the warriors cut their thongs, giving them buckskin shirts, leggings and moccasins, and escorted them back to their tepee. "They must be savin' us for somethin' special," said the sergeant.

"You must mean me," said the lieutenant. "I'm the one who he thinks killed his son."

"I did," said the sergeant.

"I was in charge," went on the lieutenant, "so I'm responsible." They were quiet. Behind them the dogs began to lick the bloody ground.

They slept, exhausted. In the morning they were awakened by the shouts of children playing in the sun in front of the tepee. A warrior came and relieved Haysoos. Beth sat up and tried to throw her loose hair into place by tossing her head back. The children had collected a handful of grasshoppers and were busily tying them together two by two; they then set them down. The grasshoppers jumped frantically in different directions at once, and the first one that was overturned lost for its owner. After they played that for a while they made little arrows, with the grasshopper legs for points; they inserted the legs into reeds and played hunter until they got tired of that.

Then a little boy lay on his back; another got between his legs and pulled him in a circle, smoothing the rough sand in front of the tepee. One of the children stood in the center of the circle with his shoulders hunched over like a bear's; the others placed their hands on the hips of the one in front and so the chain moved until the bear succeeded in pulling someone out of the chanting and shuffling circle. Then that one became the bear. Once an old man walking by was persuaded to enter the circle and he let himself be pulled out of line, and becoming the bear, made them scream in delight with his heavy and realistic grunting.

They finally tired of their games and peered into the tepee; one of Kicking Bird's fat squaws came by and shooed them away but they came back like floating gulls after the passage of a heavy ship, and stared at the prisoners. The little boy turned to the warrior and asked, "Will they become Comanches?"

The warrior said he did not think so. He said the other white men did not die well. "One of them cried, and the other was too scared. These will die well. And the woman is worth many horses."

"How many?"

"Oh, many, many."

Then the little girl came in and sat down. She pushed aside Beth's long hair and stared at her blue eyes, fascinated. She stroked Beth's face and the two men watched, smiling.

"Ask her for a knife," said the sergeant, grinning.

"No," said the lieutenant. "Don't let anyone know you know Comanche."

The little girl peered closely at Beth's face. She announced, "Her eyes are the color of bluebonnets!" The other children wanted to look, too, but just then one of Kicking Bird's squaws came in and said, "Go away!" The little girl left sullenly. "There is not much meat left," the squaw went on. "I am glad the men are going tomorrow." The warrior grunted. It was obvious he did not like her; she stooped heavily and left the tepee.

Sergeant Christie said, "Did you hear that?"

Beth nodded. The lieutenant asked, "What's up?"

"We're going someplace tomorrow," said the sergeant. "And she stays here. My guess is we're gonna be showed off in a few villages. That's to show how brave Kicking Bird was to take us. And when they use up all the villages . . ."

When it grew dark, a man outside built three small fires in a row, then he slowly began walking a pony near them, back and forth, back and forth for hours. After a few minutes the lieutenant asked, "What's that for?"

"Toughen up the hooves," said the sergeant.

They forced themselves to sleep.

Toward eight o'clock they were awakened by thunder.

Sgt. Christie turned to Haysoos, who was sitting opposite, watching warily. "Do they let you kill buffalo?" asked the sergeant.

Haysoos was furious. He said that was a foolish question. He said everyone knew Comanche warriors learned how to kill buffaloes before they were fourteen. Sergeant Christie was chastened. He asked humbly for the best way to kill buffaloes. Haysoos was happy at the prospect of telling someone something; above all, someone who would not leave in the middle of his recital—a regretful habit indulged in by many of the warriors.

"You ride behind and on his left," he began. "You drive the arrow downward and toward his heart. It goes right into the heart . . ." On he went. The sergeant kept feeding him questions whenever he seemed on the point of slowing down.

The thunder had stopped. In the sudden silence they could hear the great thrashing of the cottonwoods in the wind. Then the rain began; it beat hard upon the tepee and it seemed as if it would last all night. There was no chance Haysoos would fall asleep—he slept most of the day to prepare himself for the night watch—and from time to time he interrupted the sergeant's questions and his own boasting to toss another log on the fire so he could see what the prisoners might be doing.

Lt. Stowe asked: "Think of anything yet?"

"Nope," replied the sergeant. "I'm workin' on it."

The sergeant asked Haysoos, "Do you have your own carbine?"

Haysoos said sadly, "Yes. Not a very good one. I could have a better one if I took one on a war party. Or I could buy one for three good buffalo ponies."

"Why don't you?"

"My father gave me only one horse," he said. "A bad pony. It is old and no good." He lowered his voice. "My father is stingy," he said, aggrieved. "But I have a very good one now," he added, pleased. "Perhaps you saw me setting the fire before our attack on you. Soon I will have more carbines, and already I am trusted to guard prisoners."

Sergeant Christie pointed to a long buckskin bag hanging from a lodge pole. "What's in there?" he asked casually.

Haysoos said his father's carbine used to be there.

"Used to be?"

"When you were coming," said Haysoos, "he moved it to another tepee. Those are arrows in the bag now."

"Well, goddam your old man," said the sergeant, in English.

"No comprendo," said Haysoos, puzzled.

"Look, I don't want to talk any more," said the sergeant. Haysoos sulked.

"I got it!" said Sgt. Christie, suddenly breaking the silence.

Haysoos looked puzzled, since the sergeant had spoken in English. The sergeant went on, in Comanche: "I want to relieve myself."

Haysoos rose, drew his knife, and walked over. He checked the wrist and ankle thongs of everyone. Satisfied, he kneeled and untied the sergeant's ankle thongs.

"Get up!" he said, and motioned for him to rise. Christie drew back his legs and suddenly kicked out. His right heel caught Haysoos' jaw and there was a dull click. Haysoos lay unconscious. With his bound hands the sergeant picked up Haysoos' knife and cut Lt. Stowe's wrist thongs. In less than a minute they were all unbound. The tepee door, however, was open to the view of any curious passer-by, and they had to work fast.

They shoved a calico rag in Haysoos' mouth, and bound it in place with another one. Then they cut down a few buckskin bags and arranged them; a quick look might convince someone looking in casually that there were three bodies lying still.

The sergeant cut down a bag from the rafters; it contained buckskin shirts and leggings. "Put 'em on fast," he said. "Put 'em on right on top." They did, and he pulled down the bag with the arrows; a bow was also in the same bag. The lieutenant took it; then the sergeant made a slit in the tepee wall, quite low. They crawled through; on the way out the sergeant pulled a buckskin bag in front of the slit to hide it. It was dark and raining hard, and no one was in sight.

"Oh, my God!" said the sergeant, "I forgot saddles." He started to go back, but the lieutenant grabbed him. "Too late," he whispered.

"Sorry, Lieutenant," said the sergeant, stubbornly. "I know I'm in the cavalry, but I ain't gonna ride back three hundred miles bareback on these sharp-boned Indian ponies." He went back and dragged out three saddles and bridles. "We're makin' Kicking Bird a poor man," he said, grinning. Shouldering the saddles they walked boldly between the tepees. "Don't crawl, and don't hold your heads down," advised the sergeant.

In three minutes they arrived at the horse herd. Two boys, each of Haysoos' age, were on guard. They stared, curious, at the three approaching figures, and one asked, "Who are you?"

Sgt. Christie said loudly in Comanche, as if he were drunk, "Where is my pony? We want to see my pony!"

The guards laughed. They got within ten feet when the other guard said, "Who are these men? I do not know them."

Before he could lift his carbine, the sergeant threw the knife he had taken from Haysoos. The guard dropped his carbine and clutched at the hilt sticking from his throat. The other guard flung open his robe and grabbed his tomahawk. He had raised it to throw when Christie hit him in a hard tackle at knee-level. He fell backward into a puddle of rainwater and Lt. Stowe swung the carbine by the barrel and hit him with the butt. He lay still, his face in the water. The lieutenant dragged him out. Christie searched the other for cartridges. He found one. "Dammit!" he said. He raised the tomahawk.

"No," said the lieutenant.

"What?" he said, amazed.

"Tie him, that's all."

"He'll only come against us tomorrow."

"One more won't make that much difference," said the lieutenant. "And why didn't you kill Haysoos?"

"Well, the kid's so dumb I sorta liked him. And I liked that ride he made."

The boy with the knife in his throat tried to raise up; he gurgled, and fell back, dead.

"Tie him and let's go," the lieutenant said.

"Do you mind, sir, if I do a good job on him?"

"By no means, Sergeant."

The sergeant did a good job. Then they caught three horses and saddled them. The direct course to Fort Brill lay southeast, as well as they could judge. "We'll ride west," said the lieutenant, "and after a day we'll begin to circle around to the southeast." They set off at a sharp trot.

After an hour it stopped raining; the clouds broke open and the moon shone out. The sergeant cursed softly. But it was a crescent moon and on its back. They looked at it, content: the Comanches rarely left on a raiding party when the moon was crescent and in that position; it was full and running over, and that meant more rain, and that, in turn, meant that their trails might be washed away, if it rained hard enough.

It did not mean that there would be no pursuit from Kicking Bird's village, but the rain might delay them and the chances of running across a raiding party from another Comanche village were lessened. And once more it began to rain.

EIGHTEEN

In the village someone noticed the slit in the back of the tepee after sunrise. Kicking Bird ran heavily to the tepee and watched Haysoos being unbound. "Fool!" he said. He tried to persuade many warriors to ride in pursuit with him, but they were tired after the night's dancing and the long raid they had been on. They saw no profit in going on such a pursuit: the horses would go back to their original owners, and Kicking Bird would not permit scalps to be taken, since he wanted to torture Stowe for a long time. Christie was destined for the same, and Beth was to be traded for horses and rifles. They had sufficient glory and loot from their last raid. Besides, it was raining. Only seven were willing to ride with Kicking Bird, and Haysoos asked to come.

The prisoners had a head start of several hours. The heavy rains had washed away their tracks, and when Kicking Bird started in pursuit he assumed the general trail would lie to the southeast, the way they had come. They rode for hours in that direction before Kicking Bird called a halt. Even with the heavy rain, there should have been some sign by that time: a freshly-snapped bough, an overturned stone, some horse droppings. There was nothing.

They rode back to the village, and through it, and Kicking Bird's refusal to let them stop for a hot meal angered them, and three men dropped out. Kicking Bird led the others, ranging back and forth in long arcs, looking for sign, and after three hours he found droppings, several hours old, from a horse that had been walking. It could not be a wild horse, for they always stopped to relieve themselves. This was the trail, then, and they settled down in pursuit.

Ahead Lt. Stowe and Sgt. Christie hoped that the fact that they had ridden for six hours at a right angle from the course the Comanches thought they would follow would throw pursuit off their trail; the all-night rain would wipe out their pony tracks. But they wished to make sure, and it was noon before they halted. By then the sun had come out strongly, and when the lieutenant looked at Beth's face, he said, "Let's take a break."

They reined in and let the horses crop the damp grass. The lieutenant took off his outer buckskin shirt and hung it on a bush to dry in the sun; then he took his inner shirt and spread it out for Beth to lie upon. She curled up and fell asleep immediately. The two men sat and looked at their weapons. They had a sheath knife, a bow and a quiver of hunting arrows, and a new Winchester with the name "D. Dewhurst, Canon Escondido, Arizona" burned into the stock. There were six cartridges in it. Sergeant Christie searched for a rag to clean it, and his eyes fell on Beth's cavalry shirt.

Lt. Stowe noticed it at the same time. He squatted beside Beth, and brushed back her hair, which had fallen in a black cloud and covered one side of her face. She woke, startled, but seeing him, smiled sleepily. He began to pull out her shirt. She smiled again, slowly, warmly, and sleepily, and held out her arms. "No, no," said the lieutenant, blushing, "it's for the carbine." Christie pretended he had not noticed this byplay.

He ejected the cartridges, set them very carefully one by one on his shirt, which he had also taken off to dry; then he started to take apart the carbine. In the meantime the lieutenant unwrapped the bow and arrows and looked at them helplessly.

"Do you know anything about these things?" he asked. The sergeant shrugged. "All I know is they're made of Osage orange and you can kill a buffalo better with one than a bullet, but I never held one of the damn things." Twenty feet away grew a small willow with a foot thick trunk. The lieutenant rose, awkwardly fitted an arrow and let it go. He missed the trunk by five feet, and the arrow and bow slipped down in his hand till he grasped the end of it; then he drew back his arm, preparing to sling it into the sagebrush.

"Keep it, Lieutenant," said the sergeant, "it may come in handy."

"You saw what happened—can you do better?"

"Nope, but keep it anyways. Beth ain't bad at it at all. All we got is six cartridges to take us over three hundred miles, the way I work it out. And we gotta fight on those. The arrows are for food, and we gotta use 'em even if we gotta creep up on the game and stab 'em to death with the arrows." He finished wiping the damp parts, then he assembled them while the lieutenant practiced bending the bow. Then the sergeant kissed each cartridge as he shoved it into the magazine. He patted the trigger, then wrapped the carbine in its buckskin cover.

"We better start movin'," he said. They woke up Beth, who stood up and mounted her horse sleepily. They looked for game as they rode, but all they saw was a golden-fronted woodpecker drumming for grubs among some dead oaks low on a rocky slope.

They forded a cold shallow creek, climbed the other slope, and Christie, in the lead, held up his hand. A few hundred yards away several hundred buffalo were running hard towards the south through the grass. The sergeant did not move.

"Let's go take a look-see," he said, "why they're runnin!" They rode through a soggy bit of grassland, then up a sand hill; at the top were three fresh pony tracks. "Oh, oh," he said. "Let's get out of here fast."

They slid down the hill and headed west, away from the herd. They trotted quickly around the foot of the hill and almost ran full tilt into two Comanches on buffalo ponies. The ponies were panting and sweating. The sergeant's carbine was still wrapped in its buckskin cover. No one moved.

Two hundred yards away, a buffalo cow lay dying, an arrow sticking out of its side; behind it lay a dead calf, beside it stood a patient pony. Skinning it was another Comanche, who stood up and stared at them, a dripping knife in one hand. None of the Comanches was carrying a carbine; only bows and arrows.

The sergeant unwrapped his carbine quickly and shot one of the Comanches through the heart. The other wheeled his horse and took off at a full gallop, sliding down on one side till only his head and foot were visible. The sergeant spurred after him. The figure skinning the buffalo had mounted its pony at the sound of the shot, but after a few paces the pony stumbled and sent it sprawling. It was on its feet in a second, and as the Comanche went by he pulled the skinner up behind him at full gallop.

Sgt. Christie fired. The moment he did so he realized the figure was a woman. The bullet went through her body and was stopped by the quiver of arrows slung over the man's back. The woman, clasping her husband by the waist, died and slid off, pulling him to the ground with her. He landed, running, spun around, and loosed an arrow. It went into the shoulder of the sergeant's horse, who began bucking in pain. The Comanche kept shooting arrows, and the sergeant fired from the pitching horse and broke the Comanche's right elbow. He could not use his bow any more, and let it drop. With his left arm he pulled his knife from its sheath.

The sergeant's horse became quiet, and he fired again, hitting the Comanche in the chest. He turned and walked to a dead tree nearby, leaned against it, and began singing his death song. The sergeant rode up and the Comanche kept thrusting weakly at him with his knife. The lieutenant said, "End it, end it!" The sergeant fired once more and the Comanche slid down the trunk of the tree, dropping his head on his chest.

They wheeled their horses, caught the Comanches' horses, and headed at a fast trot to the dead buffalo. The dead squaw had already cut out the ribs and the tongue. They picked it up and healed east at a fast trot. Most likely there were more Comanches out hunting, and they had to leave fast. In the middle of the afternoon they shifted to the captured horses; all afternoon they rode hard.

Two hours before sunset they halted, built a small fire of buffalo chips, and broiled the tongue. They were so hungry that the three of them ate most of it. As soon as they ate they rode two hours out of their general course and halted at dusk. This was done so that if their cooking fire were seen (which was not likely because buffalo dung burned almost without smoke) they would sleep as far as possible from pursuit, which would come upon the fire when it was too dark to follow their trail.

That night they hobbled the horses and slept without a fire, but whenever they thought of the trip to the Comanche village, staked down at night, it seemed a luxury to be able to turn in their sleep. They slept next to one another for warmth, and in the night Beth awoke, trembling. They lay silently looking at the stars, and then she said, "Why did you kill them, Boo?"

"Had to."

"You didn't have to," she said. "They didn't have a gun; you could have taken away their bows and arrows and let them go. They could have walked back."

The lieutenant said, "He did what I have would have done. If we let them go they would have found the rest of the hunting party or maybe Kicking Bird and come down on us."

"Maybe," said the sergeant, "and maybe in the excitement they would have gotten one or more of us with them arrows. Comanches don't surrender so easy. But things got out of hand. Maybe I got a bit excited, but I couldn't see myself hangin' up in the air like Schweizer or Wheaton like a goddam fly stuck in honey. I don't like to shoot nobody, but when I figure they're gonna go for me, I go for 'em first. I ain't a Southern gentleman, and I don't fight duels. But I am sorry I got that squaw. He pulled her up so fast behind him I didn't see her skirt." He turned over, drew up his legs, tucked his hands under his armpits and tried to fall asleep.

Next morning, when Beth was saddling her pony, a hen quail drummed up out of the grass into the face of the grazing horse. She reared, terrified, and then galloped as hard as she could to the north, toward the lodges of her former owners. By the time Lt. Stowe had finished saddling his horse and had left in pursuit the frightened pony had disappeared over the ridge.

The sergeant watched them. "He ain't gonna catch that light pony," he said. "The only chance he got to get her is if she stops to graze some, and she was so scared she looked like she was gonna run all day."

Half an hour later the lieutenant came back. He did not have the escaped pony in tow. He dismounted, worried.

Beth said, "I'm very sorry."

"It doesn't matter," he said. "That could've happened to any one of us."

"Don't worry about it," said the sergeant. "It don't matter. We still got us each one to ride. I don't like to say this and I could be wrong, but Kickin' Bird don't need to backtrack over trail to find us, with us leavin' sign the way we are. All I hope is that big rain the night we took off washed away our tracks. Anyway, let's get goin'."

Beth was trembling. The lieutenant patted her back, and Christie awkwardly stroked her hair.

In a few moments she quieted down. "Boo!" she said, half-indignant, half-amused, "you touch me like I'm a horse."

"You been very good up to now," he said, "very, very good."

"Better than Kitty Burton would be?"

"Oh, Lord, no comparison," he said, grinning.

They found no water and twice during the afternoon they got off course by following buffalo trails they thought would lead them to water. An hour later, far across a valley, Beth saw an antelope. The wind was blowing in their direction, and the antelope had not smelled them yet. The sergeant began to unwrap the carbine.

"Hold it," said the lieutenant, "how many cartridges you got left?"

"Two."

"We better save 'em."

"Sure we better save 'em, but we also gotta eat." He checked the chamber. "Yeah, two," he said sadly.

"Flag them, the way we used to," said Beth.

"My God, yes," said the sergeant. "That'll get him up here. And maybe at five feet or so you won't miss with the bow."

"Maybe it'll work, Boo," she said. "I used to practice for hours—remember?"

"Yeah, sure," said the sergeant, "that's it."

"What do you mean, 'flag 'em'?" asked the lieutenant.

"Watch," said Beth. They dismounted and left the horses on the other side of the ridge so that they could not be seen by the antelope.

The sergeant lay on his back near the ridge and began waving his legs back and forth. From the valley side where the antelope was grazing the only thing that could be seen of him were his legs. In the meantime Beth fitted an arrow to the bow and sat to one side of the sergeant and a few feet below the ridge line so that she, too, would be unseen by the antelope.

Far across the valley the antelope lifted his head and saw the waving buckskin legs. He stared. Then, very slowly, he moved to investigate. It took him twenty minutes to move within ten feet of the sergeant's legs. Very slowly he neared. Very slowly he poked his head over the ridge. Beth was warned of his approach by the rattle of a few loose pebbles under his hooves, and when he poked his head over the ridge she had already drawn the bow and was ready. When his throat made a good target she loosed the arrow. The antelope leaped sideward, turned, and ran a hundred feet before he collapsed.

"And that's what we call flaggin'," said the sergeant. "My legs are killin' me."

They skinned the antelope, cut steaks from it, and broiled them on the spot. They ate two pounds apiece; the rest they rolled up in the hide, and rode off course again for two hours and slept.

Far behind them, Kicking Bird's party found the escaped pony. She was not important to him now, except to confirm that he was on the trail, which had become increasingly plain. Only three were in the party now: Kicking Bird; Haysoos, who was determined to go all the way with his adopted father in order to wipe out the shame of having been tricked by the whites; and Bear Wolf, who had always been lucky on any party led by Kicking Bird. The other warriors who had come out with them had decided they would do better hunting buffalo when they saw a herd, and had ridden off. Kicking Bird and the two others with him killed the pony and ate some of the flesh. The rest they carried in their pursuit.

The next morning the escaped prisoners came upon a broad valley miles across; it was bordered on both sides by tall granite cliffs. The valley trend was to the southeast;

and the valley floor was perfectly flat, graveled and filled with sagebrush. At the foot of the cliffs were massive boulders.

"It leads our way," said the sergeant. "It looks dry as a cat's tongue, but it leads our way."

"I vote yes," said the lieutenant.

They rode in. Two hours later they made a small fire, feeling exposed as they sat in the middle of the valley floor. They ate some steak, and then the sergeant unwrapped his carbine and looked at it. "Isn't she pretty?" he murmured. "I bet D. Dewhurst was proud of her."

They rode toward the cliff face and along it till they found a small trickle sliding down the cliff face, forming a tiny pool among some boulders. There they drank.

All the rest of the day they rode into the valley. The air had the clearness and cleanliness of the west, so the great distances seemed nothing; a small butte in the center of the valley seemed only a mile away—but it took them five hours of riding to reach it.

The gravelled floor of the valley began to lame the horses, and still the valley did not end, nor did it until two days later, when it made a sharp bend to the left, or northeast, and became an arroyo filled with enormous round boulders. That night the horses had nothing to eat. The next day the walls of the valley began to close in on one another; all day the valley narrowed. That night they ate the rest of the antelope and drank from a small pool of stagnant rainwater in which buffaloes had been; they had to strain the loose buffalo hair between their teeth. That night the horses were restless and weak.

All three of them had lost weight. The last of the antelope had been eaten and their only drink was from stagnant pools in which buffaloes had waded. They could feel their hearts slam against their ribs with the slightest exertion. Through the rips in their clothing the skin was burned red wherever the sun had struck, and their lips were beginning to crack. The horses had not eaten for two days and were restless and weak. The sergeant knew how easy and how dangerous it would be to stop and to rest, here in this open, exposed plain without water or food. He knew all three of them wanted to lie down and sleep, but he knew that when they woke they would be weaker than ever. Their only chance lay in moving until they should find water and food. It was a hard and irritating task, picking their way among the boulders, and he was afraid Beth might break into hysteria, but she did not, and from time to time he turned around in his saddle and looked at her proudly.

Upward climbed the arroyo; the cliff walls grew closer, shutting out the sun. Nothing grew anywhere. The horses began to pant and gasp; their hooves were cracked. The arroyo made one more sharp bend to the east and ended in a five hundred foot wall.

Beth leaned forward in her saddle, pressing her face against the horse's neck. Her braids mingled with the black mane. Then she slid off, sat on a rock, and patted her horse, who was trembling. "We're all thirsty," she said, "all of us."

Nobody said anything more.

They turned back and had ridden for half an hour when the sergeant caught sight of something green deep inside a narrow cleft that slit the cliff wall from top to bottom. It was something they had not noticed riding in because it would been noticed only by someone looking backward. The sergeant said, "Wait a minute. I'll take a look down there." He took out the carbine and rode in. In five minutes he was back. "We found a home, Lieutenant," he said. They followed him through the gap; then along a narrow rock-strewn path and down to the left, around a shoulder of the cliff, and into a tiny box canyon.

At the foot of the cliff was a clear round pool, formed by a wall of tumbled boulders. It was constantly renewed by a tickle of water emerging from the rock face just above it. On the other side of the pool was a grove of willows whose leaves shone silver in the afternoon light against the black cliffs; at the further end of the pool was a growth of white dogwood through whose leaves the sunlight fell onto a dense growth of giant fern, and mingling with the willows and gradually increasing in number so they finally ruled the center shore was a heavy stand of pines.

Somehow the water seeped underground and formed a lower pool twenty feet down the slope. This pool was shallower and warmer than the upper one; around it grew moss and the last asters of the year.

Since here was the only water for miles, the edges of the pools were filled with deer and antelope tracks; there was plenty of grass stretching from the pool side to the other cliff bottom. The canyon ran east and west, thus placing it under the transit of the sun all day long.

That night they ate and slept well. Sgt. Christie had the morning watch, and left with the carbine and lay under the pines so that he could command the trail and yet not be seen.

Beth and the lieutenant went for fresh ferns for mattresses. She had gone earlier and had bathed in the lower pool, and as she waited for the lieutenant to bathe she braided her hair.

He came up from the pool, leaned against a willow trunk, and watched her. He brushed aside the long hanging branches of the willows so he could see better. Her hair was still damp, and it shone black and sleek as otter fur; and her uplifted arms thrust out her breasts. The top button of her shirt had been ripped off days ago, and when she noticed the lieutenant looking at her, she smiled as she braided.

He dropped the bunch of fern he was carrying and knelt beside her; he put one hand on her shoulder while with the other he cupped her left breast in his hand. Her eyes softened, and then she pressed her cheek against the hand on her shoulder; then she turned her face upward to be kissed. Her eyes were half-closed. He kissed her a long time; the scent of the pine needles drifted upward.

He pulled back a moment and looked at her. Her skin was white as the inner bark of the cottonwood, and in the half-light under the fronds of the willow it shone against the dark green of the ferns like a new moon. Then she lifted her arms high overhead into the willow fronds in a long catlike stretch.

Afterwards they went to sleep.

When they woke it was getting dark and they joined the sergeant, who was broiling venison. They ate, and then sat for a moment, looking at the fire until it was time to go on guard.

"I often think of gettin' married," said the sergeant.

"Again?" asked the lieutenant.

"Yep. The Great Western took a fancy to me. I was thinkin' why do I have to use my few pennies to open up a crummy ole 'dobe saloon near a dirty Army fort, when me and her can move out to San Francisco, say, and really have us a place with chandeliers and deep pink carpets and mirrors fifteen feet across with them fat little boys carved in gold all around them? I seen really high class places in New Orlins and I know what's good. I never been out to California and I'm curious. Maybe if she was handled right I could work it."

"But how can you marry her if you never got a divorce from your first wife?"

"She don't know that, Lieutenant, and you wouldn't be mean enough to tell her. Anyway, when we make it back I'm quittin'. I want no part of the major's winter campaign. It's gonna work, I'm sure of it, and it's gonna catch 'em when they least expect it, and when they got skinny horses, and a lot of dead braves, and when they'll have lost a lot of carbines. I've had enough of the Army, and what I want now is some easy livin'."

"When the campaign is over," said the lieutenant, "it'll be easy livin'."

"Sure, it's easy livin' bein' a truant officer," retorted Boo. "But I'd hate it. It'd be shameful to shove

Comanches around when they used to have carbines and good ponies. They'd be ashamed too. No, Lieutenant, I'm pullin' out the second my enlistment runs out. And then—hear that?" He dropped his light tone and tensed.

"You mean that whippoorwill?"

"Whippoorwills like trees," said the sergeant, softly. "This one is up in the rocks. I don't like whippoorwills who don't stay in trees." He took the carbine and said, "Keep talkin' real easy and relaxed, and keep movin' so's you'll both make bad targets. Don't let them whippoorwills get suspicious." He edged out of the fire light and was gone.

The whippoorwill called suddenly. The other one answered. The lieutenant stood up, yawned, and strolled back and forth, pretending to look for firewood while he said to Beth, quietly, "Get near to your bow and arrows."

Something brushed against Sgt. Christie's shoulder. At the same time he heard the crash of a carbine from somewhere above him. He threw himself flat, and rolled over on his back and saw an orange flame lick out of a carbine muzzle on the ridge above him. It was Kicking Bird, who had corrected his aim, and if the sergeant had not moved so quickly his head would have been smashed open by the second bullet. The sergeant shot, lying on his back.

Kicking Bird was standing now, his passion for revenge momentarily stripping him of his senses, which otherwise would have told him that with the moon at his back he was a perfect target. The bullet went into an eye and came out at the back of his skull. For a second he stood, then pitched forward off the ridge.

Two more carbines crashed. Sergeant Christie fired at one of the flashes with his last bullet, and Bear Wolf, who had come all the way with Kicking Bird and Haysoos, half rose, clutching his stomach, and sat down with a grunt, worked the lever of his carbine, and lifted it to fire at the defenseless sergeant. Suddenly he let slip the carbine and grabbed the arrow that feathered his heart. Beth had shot him.

Boo had no more bullets. No one moved. If someone could get hold of Kicking Bird's or Bear Wolf's carbine . . . Kicking Bird's carbine lay beside his body; Bear Wolf lay across his. No one knew whether or not there was a third or even more Comanches. The night was still. Occasionally the wind stirred a little in the branches of the pines.

The three whites were too far apart to whisper to one another.

Very slowly Boo placed his hat on the end of his empty carbine. Then he slid it above the edge of the boulder behind which he lay. The hat jumped off the carbine as the orange flash and roar came from the cliff. Then there was someone, and he was a good shot.

Boo picked up a stone and threw it into as high a parabola as he could. After four seconds he heard it clattering atop the ridge somewhere behind the place where the last shot had come from. As soon as he heard the stone rattle he ran, stooping, to where Kicking Bird lay on his back beside his carbine. It was hard to pull it from the dead fingers and in doing it he wasted seconds. Just as he wrenched it free he dropped: half a second later a bullet screamed through the air where his head had been. He lay flat and checked the carbine. The trigger had been snapped off in the fall.

He took out the bullets. Now he had to get back to his own carbine. He cursed himself for not having taken it with him. Feeling better after that, he picked up four small stones; two he threw far to the left, and two far to the right. As they clattered among the boulders he ran for his boulder and the carbine behind it. Once more the orange flash licked out, and this time he was hit in his left shoulder. The impact forced him to his knees, and the pain was momentarily more than that of his shoulder. Irrationally he thought of the time he had once squeezed the trigger ten years ago somewhere in Virginia, and the way the Union officer had folded across the fence, pressing his hands against his belly and screaming, high pitched, like a hurt rabbit. Boo had stood that for about five minutes. Then Boo had shot him again.

That thought took less than a second, and he was behind the boulder. He knew he had to make his shot count before the shock of his wounded shoulder wore off. He crammed the three bullets into his carbine. Another shot blew rock splinters into his face, and this time Beth loosed an arrow at the flash. The arrow went into Haysoos' upper right arm. He reached across his body to break off the shaft and Boo's bullet smashed into his left armpit. The impact turned the slight figure halfway round. He struggled to a kneeling position and Boo fired again.

This time Haysoos was hit in the small of his back. His hands dropped the good carbine that his adopted father had given him and he clawed at his shattered spine as he collapsed, screaming a word he had not spoken since he was taken from his people years before: "Ay, Mama!" He knew he did not have enough strength left to pick up and aim the carbine at the lieutenant and the sergeant, who were climbing the cliff toward him.

He pulled himself to the edge of the cliff with his elbows, and slid off.

He died as the three of them watched him. Beside him Kicking Bird lay on his back, one eye staring at them, the other eye a bloody hole. In the moonlight the bone of his amputated finger shone like a pearl.

It was a week after they had left the canyon before any of them could forget that grotesque last view of Kicking Bird. They were dressed now as Comanches and riding Indian ponies, but they knew their disguise would hardly stand the scrutiny of a stray war party.

This thought, plus the terrain and its hardships, helped dim the gruesome memories that might otherwise have overwhelmed them. There were no more great wide valleys or deep canyons. It was becoming full prairie again, with the occasional hidden ravine that suddenly opened up before them, with willow and cottonwood growing along the tiny creeks that watered them. Once in a while a ravine's presence was betrayed by the waving tops of the trees just above the prairie level.

There was not much growth of trees in the ravines they ran across; frequently there was enough cottonwood bark for the horses, but it took hours to cut it with Haysoos' knife, which was badly dulled by now. As a result the horses were only given enough to keep going, and they were always hungry.

On the eighth day they were so weak that the strength needed to cut cottonwood was beyond them; they sat their horses near the trees and let the horses eat all the twigs they could reach.

They slept badly. The next morning even mounting the horses was difficult, and they rode slumped over their saddles.

Soon afterward it began to rain. They did not feel it at first, riding huddled over their saddle horns. Once they thought they saw some Osage, but they dared not risk attracting attention: it might have been a Comanche war party, and they had no ammunition left.

It was the twenty-second day after Kicking Bird had attacked the horse herd and captured them in the valley, and they had traveled over five hundred miles, when they thought they saw Comanche lance pennants floating behind a ridge. But it was the guidons of a patrol of the Third Cavalry, led by Capt. Mason.

"Oh, Lord!" he said slowly when he reached them. "Are you all that's left?"

Beth leaned against his shoulder and began to cry. She turned her face away so that Boo and Lt. Stowe could not see it.

Boo said proudly, "She didn't cry till now. Go ahead, honey, bawl all you want."

Capt. Mason stared at the skinny figures and the fleshless cheekbones and the ribs of the played-out horses. "Let's go home," he said. Late that afternoon they saw Fort Brill in the grey mist.

The regular flag had been torn into ribbons by the recent winds and the smaller storm flag was flying. The wild geese were screaming as they flew over the fort, and a corporal saw them ride in; he ran splashing through the mud, to report to the major.

NINETEEN

The major looked out of his window. Men in yellow slickers were greasing the axles of the supply wagons. Two by two, forty mules trotted across the parade ground in the rain.

Stretching from the vertical frame of the window sill to the bottom was a small spider web. "Watch," said the major, to Lt. Stowe. "I was saving this for Wynn and you to see."

Very gently he touched the web with a pencil tip. Two small spiders ran out and crouched expectantly in the center of the web. "I called them 'Welles' lieutenants'," he said. "Yes. I'm sorry about Wynn."

He took the pencil and twisted it in the web till all the filaments were wound tightly about it, and the terrified spiders had run frantically for another hiding place. "I wouldn't let the orderly clean it away," he said. He threw the pencil in the wastebasket and sat down. "And the others. You'd best get out the letters to the next of kin."

He looked at the signed report of the horse-herd convoy. Attached to it was the statement made by the dying

Comanche that had remained intact all through the lieutenant's captivity and escape. "This is enough to hang the man," he said. "But where is Cross? Nobody knows. He said he had to go to St. Louis for supplies, and not a word from him since. St. Louis says he never showed up there. Maybe he cut out with the profits. At any rate I have appointed Pease acting agent until the official firing comes through, and then I'm sure he'll be reappointed. And I've sent out circulars to all Army posts about Cross."

Lt. Stowe said, "My guess is he's dead by now."

"What makes you think so?"

"He's probably been shot with his own carbines." He repeated to the major the Comanches' intention of killing Cross with the next delivery he was to make.

"Probably, probably," mused the major. "So he could be dead up by the Platte?"

"I think so."

"I'll ask Fort Kearney to scout around for sign of him." The major made a note. "Well, Lieutenant, thanks for taking care of Beth. I'm recommending you for a captaincy for the way you handled yourself."

The lieutenant grew red.

"Promotions take a long time to get put through on the frontier," added the major. "Especially in peace time. Now, if we had an official war on—but Beth wants to marry you right away, captaincy or no. She says she won't wait for the promotion. She says the hell with Washington. That's what I get for bringing up a daughter around cavalry sergeants. I'd like to ask Christie if he'd care to go to the Point and come out an officer but I know he'd tell me to go to hell. I've been hearing he's had enough of the Army." He shook hands with Lt. Stowe, and said, smiling, "I might as well get used to calling you Sam. Welcome to the family."

Lt. Stowe walked out, dazed. Outside he ran into Sgt. Christie, who was leaning moodily on the porch rail. "Hello, Lieutenant," he said.

"Sergeant, you can congratulate me. I'm the major's son-in-law-to-be."

"I thought so. I saw the look on your face. Major's in a good mood?"

"Yes."

"I bet he wants to ask me to go to the Point."

"How'd you know?"

"He asks me every time my enlistment is up. Did he have a bottle of bourbon on the desk?"

"Yes."

"He tries to get me drunk and then he tries to get me to sign a paper saying I'll go but I never will. I've had enough of the Third, and I think I'll tell him now."

"You didn't like the Third?"

"Naw, the Third's all right. It's just that I've had enough of Army."

"There's plenty of work still."

"I know, but I told you I don't want to go around slappin' wrists. What the hell kind of a fight would it be against them Comanches in their winter camp? The ponies all skinny and nothin' to eat but wild onions and starved horse? And the carbines they got left won't do 'em much good against the equipment we'll have. We'll be well fed, and our horses are gonna have their fodder carried along, and we'll be eatin' well, and we'll be warm, and the squaws'll still be cryin' for the warriors they lost tryin' to jump us at the bend in the river. Nope, the odds is too lopsided. No, thanks. I signed up for a soldier. So I'm pullin' out, Lieutenant, but I'll have me a free supper and breakfast from this man's Army before I turn in my Colt and my horse."

"Keep the Colt. I'll look the other way."

"I'm gonna miss you, Lieutenant."

"I'll miss you, too."

"It's been real nice, knowin' you. I'm sure glad to see you and the lady come through all right. I didn't have to have no crawlin' behind you. I stood up and walked through Texas."

"What're you going to do, Boo?"

"I dunno. Probably get married to that thing in San Anselmo. She's stickin' to me like a hungry tick on a sick kitten. Well, spring's too short around here, anyways, and I'm gettin' sick of long winters. And when you find out what Comanche counted coup on Cross, write me right away, hear? I wanna set up Old Crow for everyone when I find out and I don't care what it'll cost. And if my woman opens her yap I'll close it for her." He said the last sentence with a gloomy sort of satisfaction.

"You sound as if you can't stand her already."

"Well, that's the way it is," said the sergeant. "I think I'll go to San Anselmo and get drunk." He watched the storm flag slide down the mast. "Lettin' up, Lieutenant. I don't think I'll see the major after all. So long, Lieutenant."

"So long, Sergeant." He watched Boo walk slowly across the parade ground in his yellow slicker, his hands in his pockets and the first leaves falling from the cottonwoods and blowing across the parade ground.

TWENTY

Sierra Nevada Mountains
Auburn, California, March 18, 1878

Dear Lieutenant: After my respects to you and Beth I
thought I would tell you that I am still on top of land
yet. I have been in San Francisco a whiles but they runs
us out so we went here and I am about to leave. It is
disgusting here. Helen Thorpe had her place up the block
a ways and a little ways down they had a massage parlor
and some railroader came in every Friday on the Omaha
run and before he went up to see one of Helens girls he
came in here and had five or six shots of old crow. I kept
a bottel special for him. And since they closed down the
town you know I haven't sold a single goddamned drink
from that bottel?

I did what I told you I once did. I said take half of
whatever there is only this time if she woulda taken up
an ax I would a killed her. So she gave me half and I
went to San Francisco with four thousand of the best and
I got rolled rite away so I drifted up with the tide to
Sacramento city and I landed.

So I took up through town. They say there is twenty thousand people living there but it looks like a hundred thousand counting chinamen and all. I can't describe my wolfish look but I think I look just like I did when we was chasing buffaloe on the Cimarron, so I struck up through town and I came to a fine large building crowded with people, so I bulged right in to see what was going on. When I got in the counsel house I took a look around and I seen the most of them had bald heads so I thought to myself, I got it now—they are Indian peace commissioners so I look to see if I would know any of them, but not one.

So after a while the smartest looking one got up and said, Gentlemen, I introduce a bill to have speckled mountain trout and fish eggs imported to California to be put in the American and the Bear and the Yuba Rivers—Lieutenant, those rivers are so muddy that a tadpole could not live in them. Caused by mining—did anyone ever hear of speckled trout living in muddy water?

They should have been with us in that valley just before we was taken by them comanches—remember the good eating those trout made, Lieutenant? And the next thing was the game law, and that was near as bad as the Fish, for there ain't no game in this country as big as a mockin bird. I heard a fellow behind me ask how long has the legislature been in session and then I caught on. It wasn't Indian commissioners after all, so I slid out.

It was getting late and no place to go—I had not a red cent, so I came back here to auburn and she wasn't home, so I broke into the house and a took a few rings out of her trunk and I got enough money so I am going trapping in the Rockies. Guess who I met! Mr. Dimpdin! He is helping me with this letter, as he is going trapping with me, and we will work eastwards and see you maybe someday soon. Give my respects to the Third Cavalry and accept the same yourself.

Boo Christie

The letter was the first news anyone had of Christie since he had left Fort Brill. It arrived there four years after he had been discharged. From Fort Brill it followed Lt. Stowe to Fort Concho; it was then forwarded to Fort Bascom, in New Mexico; there the "Lieutenant" was crossed out and the word "Captain" inserted. From Fort Bascom the letter was sent to Fort Bliss, in Texas, and then to Fort Laramie, Wyoming Territory. At Fort Laramie the name sounded familiar to the company clerk. He looked up the records and added a new address: "Mrs. Samuel Stowe, Cherry Valley, New York."

For Captain Stowe was in a military cemetery in North Dakota under a stone which read:

Captain Samuel Stowe
Third Cavalry
1846-1876
Died for the Republic
Little Big Horn

On that day of his death, many Cheyenne fought with the Sioux. After it was all over, Kate Blue Bead, a Cheyenne squaw, rode among the bodies. Many years later she said, "I saw Stowe lying dead there. I had known him in the south, in Kansas. While I was looking at him some Sioux men came and were about to cut up his body. I made sign for 'he is a friend of mine,' but telling nothing more of him. So the Sioux men only cut off one joint of a finger. Two Cheyenne women then came by. They recognized him from Kansas and they got off and pushed the point of a sewing awl into each of his ears, deep into his head. This was done to improve his hearing, as it seemed he had not heard what our chiefs told him when he smoked the peace pipe with them. They told him that if ever afterward he should break the peace promise and fight the Cheyenne the Everywhere Spirit would surely cause him to be killed.

"Many a time I have thought of him as the handsome man I saw in the south. And I have often wondered if, when I was riding among the dead where he was lying, my pony may have kicked dirt on his face."

But there was a son. He showed entirely too much interest in water, thought Major Welles, who made a yearly visit east to see him and Beth. The major had deep and troubling fears lest he wind up at Annapolis, as some idiotic uncle had suggested. On his yearly visit the major made sinister references to the danger of living near water with a strong and active son.

Beth did not find Sam's loss so bad except in the spring, when everything seemed to conspire to remind her of him. Then the tightly packed buds of dogwood opened so quickly one after the other after one or two warm days that the dusky white stars seemed to explode everywhere on the valley farm. This happened at the time when the cottonwoods with their millions of tiny opening buds along that western river seemed to float in a green haze. This was the time when the first white cranes came flying north from Mexico, and when the violets, in Cherry Valley as in Texas, began to appear in the most hidden places: between the spokes of a discarded wagon wheel back of Fort Brill's blacksmith shop, in the soil-filled crevices of great granite boulders in the distant ranges, and in the rib cage of Lt. Wynn, where, deep in the tall grass, their brilliant blue grew among the weatherbeaten shafts of three war arrows.

Summer, in turn, was more bearable. Unlike the unfolding spring it held little resemblance to Texas. The rich and gracious valley never had the dust-storms or the oven-heat that made the mesas quiver in a heat haze; and there were sunflowers back of the house, but small ones, not like the great yellow suns that soared upwards from the river bank below Fort Brill.

Autumn was soon over, but September brought the apples that the lieutenant once said had white flecks on them like young deer.

And winter: winter was when they had been married.

In the beginning Beth thought that time and young Sam would do the trick. But time had played her false; the ache was still there. Time, the cheat, had not dulled the edge of it, which was sharp enough to rise like the river each spring when the great lilac beside the kitchen door burst into bloom.

Well, enough. She had a letter to write.

JOHN BALL
AUTHOR OF **IN THE HEAT OF THE NIGHT** INTRODUCING, **POLICE CHIEF JACK TALLON** IN THESE EXCITING, FAST-PACED MYSTERIES.

FREE!!
BOOKS BY MAIL
CATALOGUE

BOOKS BY MAIL will share with you our current bestselling books as well as hard to find specialty titles in areas that will match your interests. You will be updated on what's new in books at no cost to you. Just fill in the coupon below and discover the convenience of having books delivered to your home.

PLEASE ADD $1.00 TO COVER THE COST OF POSTAGE & HANDLING.

- -

BOOKS BY MAIL

**320 Steelcase Road E.,
Markham, Ontario L3R 2M1**

**210 5th Ave., 7th Floor
New York, N.Y., 10010**

Please send Books By Mail catalogue to:

Name _____
            (please print)

Address _____

City _____

Prov./State _____ P.C./Zip _____

(BBM1)